THE MYSTERY OF HONG KONG'S PIRATE ISLAND

The Hip-Hop Twins Mysteries are light-hearted fantasy stories all based in Hong Kong, providing local readers a definite sense of identity and foreign readers an extra dimension of intrigue.

Hilton and Cookie solve mysteries and fight crime while holding themselves to a high level of civic and moral responsibility.

The Hip-Hop Twins are role models for the youth of today in Hong Kong and all other countries around the world. The Hip-Hop Twins mystery series provides entertainment as well as an opportunity to learn and improve the young reader's English language skills.

Have fun reading these thrilling tales and before you know it, you to will be part of Cookie and Hilton's HIP-HOP NATION.

G. Stuart Nakay is a native of Vancouver, Canada, now residing in Hong Kong.

The Hip-Hop Twins Mystery Series
Book One

THE MYSTERY OF HONG KONG'S PIRATE ISLAND

by

G. Stuart Nakay

EvolutionXs MultiMedia Concepts Limited

THE MYSTERY OF HONG KONG'S PIRATE ISLAND

© 2007 G. Stuart Nakay

Publishing by New Generation Publishing
2 London Wall Buildings,
London EC2M 5UU

www.newgeneration-publishing.com

Cover illustration by Justo Cascante III
Map illustration Jasmine Lau Yan Ki
Typeset in Adobe Garamond by Alan Sargent

Printed in UK by Lightning Source

Chapter 1

COOKIE CHAN, a tall, slender, attractive, fifteen-year-old girl, bounded down the stairs, two at a time, hitting the bottom with a resounding thud. She was sporting a Hong Kong Windsurfing Club baseball cap with her trademark gold and chestnut ponytail sprouting out the back. She always had a smile on her face and a sparkle in her eye. Dressed in sporty summer attire, Cookie was off to Stanley Beach with her family to see her twin brother Hilton compete in a windsurfing competition.

'Where is everybody?' she asked loudly. 'We're going to be late. Come on, let's go!'

Her mother, Robyn Chan, appeared from the kitchen with Cookie's brother Markus. Markus was the youngest in the family, typically spoiled, and full of energy. Today he seemed unusually quiet.

Robyn put her hand on Markus's forehead and looked at Cookie.

'I don't think we can make it, Markus has a little fever and maybe I will have to take him to the doctor later,' explained Robyn.

Cookie slipped her backpack over her shoulders, bent down and gave Markus a stern look. She put her fingertips on his forehead.

'What fever? Well Mister Troublemaker, how come you are such a big baby today? Are you two years old?'

'I am eight years old,' replied Markus.

'Where is Dad?' asked Cookie.

'Your father is working on a very important case and he had to go to the office early this morning,' replied Robyn. 'I guess you're on your own today. Tell Hilton we're sorry we couldn't make it. We'll all be there for the championship next week on Cheung Chau. Okay . . . you go . . . go on . . . don't be late.'

'No problem mom, I'll tell him,' said Cookie as she opened the door and stepped outside. She took out her mobile phone and started dialling.

'I have to hurry now. I'll call Echo and Sammie. Hopefully we can meet at the bus station and all go to Stanley together. Bye Mom . . . bye Markus . . . get better fast, I'm bringing home your favourite ice cream,' teased Cookie.

Robyn stood by the front door and watched Cookie walk out to the road.

'Bye Cookie, and wish Hilton good luck, and tell him to be careful,' added Robyn.

Cookie headed down the street, mobile phone to her ear waiting for Echo to answer. She put her hand in the air to signal goodbye. Markus ran to the open door and waved goodbye along with his mother.

Stanley Beach was teeming with action. Sunbathers were enjoying the warm weather, and small children were playing in the sand. Many others on the beach were engaged in various sporting activities such as volleyball, badminton, and football. It was a glorious day and there were many interested spectators curious to see what all the fuss was about. An area of the beach had been sectioned off to keep the swimmers from venturing into the waters being used by the sailboarding competitors.

Today the wind would be of paramount importance, the star of the show so to speak. The Hong Kong Windsurfing Club was having their annual regatta and the competition would be fierce. This contest was the second to last event on the calendar. The final event would be held next weekend on Cheung Chau. A large banner announcing HONG KONG WINDSURFING CLUB — CHAMPIONSHIP SERIES hung above the contestants who were checking their sailboards, making last-minute preparations. The judges were all seated at an elevated table with binoculars in hand. This contest would be judged on completing the course in a specified time range, board control, and tricks consisting of turns and jumps.

A voice on the public address system announced the beginning of the competition: Welcome to Stanley Beach for the Hong Kong Windsurfing Club Championship Series. We wish all the competitors good sailing and good luck. Competitors ready . . . first competitor, number 244, Rico Wong.

Hilton Chan, Cookie's twin brother, was a tall, handsome boy. He wore a pair of mirrored sunglasses, and an electric-blue baseball cap. His wet suit was rolled down to his waist and his short-sleeved plaid shirt was open in the front, partially displaying his athletic build. His eyes followed Rico Wong as he was towed out to the starting point. Hilton stood on the beach observing the action with his two best friends, Zack and T-Rex. Zack's baby face appearance made him look younger than he really was. He was a computer wiz and a self-proclaimed trivia expert. In his own words, Zack knew a little about everything but not a lot about anything in particular. T-Rex was big, strong, and very muscular. To outsiders, T-Rex was a very tough guy, someone you should never mess with. T-Rex liked to read science fiction comics and had a keen interest in electronic gadgets, like mobile phones, Palm Pilots, and especially game consoles like the PlayStation and X-Box. Hilton, T-Rex, whose real name was Truman, and Zack had been best friends since Primary 1. All three young men were very easy going, good natured, teenagers who were very competitive and well liked.

Hilton gave Truman the nickname T-Rex because when he got mad his nostrils flared and his face would turn ten shades of purple while he let out very fierce snarls. The three boys always looked out for each other. Cookie called them the Three Musketeers, one for all and all for one. They were all expecting a very exciting day, but they could not possibly have guessed what was in store.

Rico Wong considered himself the best at everything. He was not shy about shooting his mouth off at school, boasting about his accomplishments. Rico was all about himself. A team player he was definitely not! Hilton and Rico had been competing with each other on every level all their lives. Whether it was basketball, football, the swim team, or ping pong, Rico wanted to show everyone he was the star. Only one problem. Hilton Chan kept getting in his way, stealing his thunder, spoiling his moment of fame, and Rico did not appreciate it. Here they were again.

Hilton and his friends found Rico's cocky, loudmouth, over-confident persona really annoying. Hilton didn't care if he lost to anyone else, but there was no way he was going to lose to Rico. One of Hilton's goals in life was to beat Rico at everything, just to shut him up, though even that never lasted too long. This wasn't easy because, although Hilton hated to admit it, Rico was very good at all sports and a tough guy to beat. It all came down to who had more heart, who wanted it more.

'Let's see what you got today brother,' Hilton muttered to himself.

Rico appeared calm out in the water, waiting for the right time to begin his run. He caught a perfect gust of wind, and stood up smartly. The competition was underway. Rico's moves were smooth, effortless, and without error. He looked calm, relaxed and in control.

'Rico looks pretty good today,' said T-Rex, peering through a small pair of binoculars.

Hilton studied Rico's every move through his mirrored sunglasses. His concentration was intense.

'You only need a few points today Hilton. Rico can't even catch up to you in the final next week,' noted Zack. 'This championship is all yours brother, no problem.'

Hilton finally broke his silence.

'Looks like Rico has really found the zone today. I mean he's good, but today he's really good,' remarked Hilton. 'I don't know what he ate for breakfast, but whatever it was, it's working.'

'He's just lucky, caught the right gust of wind. He

needs luck more than you. You have all the skill, man. No problem champ, you know your technique is better and you've got more skill. Just relax — stay cool,' advised T-Rex.

The three boys watched intently as Rico finished his routine. Rico rode his board to the beach and his friends, family, and fellow competitors, gave him a rousing round of applause for a tremendous effort. Hilton clapped loudly, while Zack and T-Rex limited their appreciation to a sarcastic, almost silent, slow clap. They waited patiently to see the results.

The 'low points scoring system' was being used for this event, meaning the best performance would receive the fewest points. The competitor with the lowest number of total points in all categories would be declared the winner. The scores were presented. Rico was awarded a total of four points and the temporary number-one position, which drew a united 'Whaaaaa' from the crowd.

'Very impressive,' Hilton said to himself. He knew Rico's performance would be hard to beat. Rico had thrown down the gauntlet to everyone: Come and get me! Hilton had a few surprises on tap and relished the challenge. He had an advantage though, being the final competitor he got to watch all the others. This would allow him to muster more self confidence and formulate a winning strategy, he hoped.

Rico looked back at the scoreboard, raised his fist in the air, and gave out a loud yelp of triumph. He walked over to Hilton grinning confidently.

'Looks like you got your work cut out for you today, doesn't it, old boy,' quipped Rico, nudging

Hilton as he walked by. Rico was joined by his supporters, patting him on the back and looking in Hilton's direction, laughing excitedly.

T-Rex took one step towards Rico, but Hilton grabbed his arm, stopping him. T-Rex gave Rico's entourage a menacing glare.

'Forget it, he's always like that. Thinks he is better than he really is, better than everyone else. Talk is cheap. Let him have his few minutes of glory,' commented Hilton. 'I still have a few tricks up my sleeve.'

The event moved along and finally the announcement Hilton had been waiting for all afternoon blared over the PA system. Next competitor, number 328, Hilton Chan. Hilton very coolly took off his shirt and zipped up his wet suit. He removed his cap exposing his stylish, spiked hair and handed his clothing to T-Rex.

'Boys . . . it's show time,' said Hilton confidently as he adjusted his sun goggles, grabbed his board, and jogged towards the water.

'Show 'em how it's done cowboy,' shouted Zack. 'Ride that wind.'

Hilton waded into the shallow water and was towed out to the starting point. He waited patiently for the signal to proceed. He was hopeful the wind would be in his favour. Zack and T-Rex clapped their hands with extra vigour, looking in the direction of Rico's group, purposely to show their displeasure with Rico's, unsportsmanlike attitude.

'C'mon Hilton, let's show these guys,' shouted T-Rex. He continued to clap his hands loudly.

'Yeah, yeah, let's go buddy, you're the man,'

yelled Zack. T-Rex and Zack turned together as they heard a voice from behind.

'Where's Hilton?' said Cookie out of breath. 'Is he finished already?'

Echo and Sammie, Cookie's best friends, ran up behind her. Echo was a mathematics genius and her stylish glasses gave her a very intellectual look. She was smaller than Cookie, and very enthusiastic. Sammie had that model look, tall, slender, with an eye for fashion, using more makeup than her two friends, and always dressed for the occasion.

The boys pointed out to the ocean where Hilton was getting ready to start his run.

'Is Rico finished already?' asked Cookie.

T-Rex shook his head and Zack said, 'He's finished all right, and his programme was unbelievable.'

'You're kidding, he's such an idiot,' replied Cookie.

'I think he's kind of cute,' said Sammie.

'Rico is a jerk,' replied Echo. 'He's always teasing the girls at school. Always wants attention.'

'He's the biggest baby,' added Cookie.

Sammie shrugged. Cookie glanced over at Rico and his friends, who were looking at them and making comments which Cookie was unable to hear. Cookie stuck out her tongue at them in a very childish manner and Rico's group all started laughing and pointing their fingers at her. Cookie turned her back on them and looked out towards Hilton.

'Here we go,' said Zack.

Everyone watched as Hilton stood up on his

sailboard.

Cookie grabbed the binoculars that were still around T-Rex's neck. The strap jerked his neck slightly and he pretended to be choking.

'Hey, you're ripping my head off little sister, where's yours?' said T-Rex as he pulled the strap over his head to let Cookie have the glasses.

'In my pack,' replied Cookie. Echo unzipped the backpack and took the binoculars out. T-Rex held out his hand expecting Echo to give them to him, but no such luck. She shared them with Sammie so they could watch Hilton. T-Rex shook his head and Zack smiled. They both shaded their eyes from the sun to watch Hilton show off his sailing talents.

Hilton was up and caught a nice gust. He guided his board through the calm waters like a professional. His technique was far superior to anyone his age at the club but this was only his second year so lacked in experience. Rico had been in the club one year longer, and practised more often as lived closer to the beach than Hilton. Rico's experience had shown through today. Hilton read the wind pretty well, making minor adjustments throughout the run. His balance was excellent and he was feeling very good about his chances to do just as well as Rico or even surpass his outstanding score. The wind gods seemed to be on his side today as well. He travelled keenly through the water, cutting the waves like a hot knife through butter. He felt like he was floating at high speed over the clouds, confident in his ride. He could feel the wind picking up and realised this was his chance to silence Rico and his loudmouth friends. Hilton leaned way back on the board to create the leverage necessary to catch the wind just right. He needed more speed in order to set up his final trick. The one he had been practising all summer. The trick that he knew would win him the club championship. The trick no one else had the skill or the guts to attempt. Hilton felt the moment was near and readied for his finale. A hundred metres directly behind Hilton, a massive shadow lurked beneath the surface. The darkness moved swiftly towards Hilton, zeroing in on his position. Hilton was focused on the task at hand, unaware of any danger. The shadow advanced quickly, now only 20 metres away and closing in fast. A titanic beast accelerated upwards. The one-tonne killing machine had its next victim in sight and was about to deliver a deadly strike. A gigantic, triangular dorsal fin broke the surface and pushed forward, creating a wave powerful enough to knock Hilton off balance. The unexpected turbulence surprised Hilton and he had to struggle to keep his balance and stay on course.

'Huh, hey what happened? What's that?' said Cookie, as she adjusted her eyes to combat the bright sunlight. 'I must be seeing things. It can't be.'

Hilton leaned back, adjusting to a sudden change in wind direction. He had no idea what was happening. Out of nowhere his sailboard lifted itself out of the water. For a split second, Hilton's concentration was diverted to the floor of his sailboard. He wondered if he had hit something in the water that took him off course. He looked down, turned his head to the left, and came eye to eye with the ocean's ultimate eating machine. The most feared predator on the planet was fully exposed just below the waterline. The monster's pitch-black eyes stared right at Hilton, hypnotising him for a moment. Hilton froze as the jaws of the beast opened. Rows of razor-sharp teeth gleamed like a thousand polished daggers in the midday sun. The mere size and scope of the animal was difficult to accept. The creature appeared to be at least twice the length of his sailboard and three times as wide. He could hear his heart pounding, faster and faster, seemingly about to explode from his chest. His knees weakened to the point of collapse. It took all his strength to hold onto the sail. The shark surfaced, eyes rolled back, signalling a readiness to attack. Hilton's instinctive reflexes pulled the sail hard to the right to avoid the collision. The surging underwater killer came out of the water narrowly missing the board, only brushing up against it. The shark's miscalculated lunge created a powerful wave propelling the sailboard swiftly in the opposite direction, away from the point of attack.

Hilton knew his life was in extreme danger. The competition was forgotten. It was now a matter of life and death . . . his life and death. Hilton only had one thing on his mind. Get out of there . . . NOW!

Chapter 2

HILTON VEERED TO THE RIGHT, then to the left, hoping to throw off the sea devil's attack. He was in a race for his life. He had to get to shore fast. Hilton kept close watch on the water behind and beneath him. The blood vessels on his forehead were pulsating with every throbbing heartbeat. Staying calm under these circumstances was almost impossible but Hilton knew it was the only way he could survive.

'Control yourself, think fast, be ready,' he reminded himself. Relying upon all his sailboarding skills he took a deep breath and a made a beeline for shore.

'Has he gone crazy out there?' asked T-Rex, watching intently, shading his eyes from the sun.

'This is a disaster,' said Cookie. 'What's he doing?'

'He's heading for shore, let's go,' replied Zack.

T-Rex looked over at Rico's group and they were all staring in amazement at Hilton's erratic manoeuvres. Rico looked over at T-Rex, smiled and shrugged.

They all started running to the end of the beach where Hilton was heading.

Hilton looked down into the rushing surf trying to spot any signs of the underwater killer. He now had control of his board and caught a strong gust of wind which propelled him straight towards the shoreline. A hundred metres to safety. Just about there! Hilton felt the waves rise beneath him and looked behind to see the great fin once again bearing down on his position. He adjusted once again to catch the wind and made a 90-degree left turn. The swell of water lifted the board into the air. He looked down to see the rocketing shadow fly past him like a torpedo. The great fin again disappeared beneath the deep blue water. Hilton's hair was standing straight up as he flew the final 50 metres, urging his board to hurry. Once in the shallow water he jumped from his sailboard and ran, stumbling, and eventually crawling to the safety of dry land. He fell in a heap on the hot sand, breathing heavily, totally exhausted from his life threatening ordeal.

Cookie lead the charge. The small group of friends arrived at Hilton's landing place together. They all tried to talk at the same time.

'Hilton, what happened? Why did you do that?' asked Cookie.

The continuous buzz of voices made him feel dizzy and disoriented. Finally, he sat up, spat out a mouthful of water, caught his breath and tried to speak. He shook his head to relieve the tension and wiped the salt water from his eyes.

'Shark . . . shark,' gasped Hilton in a very weak tone.

'What? Get out,' said T-Rex.

'How cool,' smiled Zack. The three girls looked at the two boys in disgust and their piercing stares wiped the smiles off their faces.

'Are you okay, Hilton? The girls asked in unison.

Hilton nodded, affirming his well-being. 'I'm in

one piece, but I guess I really blew this one.'

His disappointment was obvious.

Rico and his friends strutted over to where Hilton was now sitting up. T-Rex intercepted them and looked sternly at Rico, eye to eye. Rico turned and looked at Hilton displaying his usual cocky smile.

'Too much pressure for you Hilton old man,' sneered Rico loudly.

Zack joined T-Rex and they deliberately bumped into Rico and his group, creating an unfriendly climate.

'Stop it you guys,' yelled Cookie. 'Hilton was attacked by a shark.'

Rico and his group raised their eyebrows and laughed. They backed off and started to move away. They kept giggling. 'A shark . . . that's a good one. Very creative my friend,' said Rico. 'Hard to admit I just kicked your ass today. I mean it's that simple, isn't it?'

'Just curious . . . anybody else here see a shark? I didn't see any sharks . . . boys, did you see any sharks?'

Rico's supporters shook their heads and smiled.

'I didn't think so,' added Rico turning back towards Hilton.

'Oh . . . by the way . . . we're tied for first place now. See you on Cheung Chau next weekend . . . shark boy.'

T-Rex helped Hilton up.

'Let's get outta here.'

'Did any of you guys see anything?' asked Hilton.

'I saw something,' replied Cookie. 'But the sun

was so bright and you were so far out, it was hard to tell. I looked over at the judges and I didn't hear any comments from them. I guess they didn't see anything either.'

'I have to tell the judges what I saw. Don't want any other swimmers or sailboarders running into that monster,' said Hilton.

'Maybe the Marine Police can fly over in the helicopter and check it out,' added T-Rex.

'Cookie . . . promise me you won't mention this to Mom and Dad . . . I mean it,' instructed Hilton. Cookie looked at her friends and did not reply.

'That big-mouth Rico is going to tell the whole school anyways,' commented T-Rex. 'You know I could suggest Rico change schools . . . he is kind of clumsy, might fall down the school stairs, have an accident or something,' he said jokingly.

'Let him talk . . . as long as it doesn't come from us,' said Hilton.

Everyone joined in and helped Hilton pack his board and equipment into the team bus. They were all hungry, except Hilton, so they headed for the Stanley Market area to get something to eat. The market was teeming with tourists eager to visit the shops and eat at the quaint and trendy restaurants. The teens turned down a narrow alley and headed towards an outdoor café located at the end of the street.

'You know what you need Hilton, a good luck charm,' said Echo.

'Yeah, that's right, good idea,' replied Sammie. Hilton looked at them and smiled.

'Yeah, maybe some super, heavy-duty shark

repellent.'

'You could use Cookie,' joked T-Rex. 'No shark would want to risk the indigestion. Can you imagine the stomach ache? Poor shark!'

'Very funny . . . ha ha ha . . . I hate you,' replied Cookie smiling.

'That's not a bad suggestion,' said Zack. 'The Hawaiians, and many other Polynesian island cultures worship the shark as a god. The shark is the king of the ocean and protects the surfers and fishermen. The Hawaiian people even used the shark to judge whether a criminal was guilty or innocent. About 500 metres off the island of Oahu, is a small island called China Hat. That 500 metres of ocean is infested with man-eating sharks. If you were accused of a serious crime, the only way to prove your innocence was to swim to China Hat and back. If the sharks didn't get you, you were set free.'

Everyone was listening intently.

'They used a shark tooth for good luck. They wore it on a string or chain around the neck. They never take it off. Those guys never went in the ocean without it. Made them fearless. The shark became their friend and protector, not their enemy.'

'Where are we going to find a shark tooth around here?' asked Hilton.

'Hey, I know where we can look,' said T-Rex excitedly.

'At the end of the market there's an old guy who sells all kinds of old junk washed up from the ocean. He has lots of neat stuff. He calls his place "the junkyard of the sea". Even if he doesn't have one, maybe he knows where we can find one.'

Hilton managed a smile. He was starting to feel a bit better.

'Why not, let's have a look,' said Hilton.

'Good idea,' said T-Rex. 'You three girls go shopping, we're going shark-tooth hunting.'

The plans for lunch were put on hold for now.

'Meet us at the restaurant in an hour,' said Hilton.

The girls waved and headed off. The boys made their way down the narrowest of market streets to an old, run-down shop. The storefront was decorated with a disorganised assortment of seafaring articles. The bins outside were full of knick-knacks made from seashells, dried starfish and seahorses, and various old, broken ship parts. The boys were rummaging through the bins when an old man emerged from the shop.

'Everything for ten dollars,' he stated cheerfully.

'Well we're looking for something special, a shark tooth,' said Hilton.

'A big one,' added T-Rex.

The old man began to smile. 'Shark tooth, big one. What kind of shark?' he asked.

The boys looked at each other, quite puzzled.

'I guess just the biggest one. Do you have any?' asked Hilton excitedly.

'Come with me,' said the old man as he led the trio inside his shop.

The old man turned on a dim light exposing piles of papers, boxes, and large containers filled with items for sale. He unlocked a back door which led to another room, more organised in appearance but very dimly lit. The boys moved around, observing some very interesting items. The old man noticed the boys' enthusiasm.

'Everything's for sale gentlemen, have a good look, don't go home disappointed or empty-handed,' he said.

'Oh . . . only one rule. You break it, you bought it.'

He took some keys from his pocket and opened the drawer of a large oak, roll top desk.

'Behold,' he said as he took out a small glass case and opened it revealing several large shark teeth.

'Wow, look at this Hilton,' said T-Rex excitedly, 'Come here!'

Zack turned quickly in response, accidentally kicking a small chest not visible on the dark floor. He stumbled awkwardly and grabbed onto Hilton to maintain his balance. Unknown to Zack, he had triggered the release of a panel on the chest and something popped out directly at Hilton's feet. Hilton wobbled under the weight of his friend and he could not avoid stepping on the object. There was a resounding CRACK!

'Looks like somebody just bought something,' said the old man, not bothering to look up.

Hilton picked up the slightly damaged, but still intact, display case. He gave it a quick glance noticing the thick layer of dust covering the small glass window made it impossible to view the contents. Hilton was more interested in what the old man had to offer and walked over to look at the collection of shark teeth. The man displayed a variety of sizes and shapes from many different types of sharks. They had never seen anything like that except on television.

'You choose one and I'll put it on a leather string for you. Then you can wear it around your neck, only take five minutes,' said the old man.

The boys examined them closely and all agreed on the largest one in the collection. This particular tooth was almost a perfect triangle, jagged along both sides, like a steak knife.

'That's a beauty,' said Zack.

'Okay . . . this one,' said Hilton. 'How much?'

'Very special price for a very special customer,' replied the old man. In an effort to bargain, Hilton held up the case he had picked up from the floor along with a small piece of the box which he had broken off. The small display case was about 20 centimetres long with glass on one side. The window box had an antique look to it and Hilton used the corner of his shirt to rub away the dusty film, exposing the contents. To his surprise it contained an old, tarnished, brass spyglass. Hilton smiled and thought the spyglass looked really cool. The old man got up from his chair, leaned over and took a look. He shrugged and scratched his head, not knowing what to make of the young man's discovery.

'How much if I buy both?' he asked with confidence.

'These shark teeth are hard to find. This is the tooth of a tiger shark, a real man-killer. Tiger sharks don't cruise into Hong Kong waters too often, kind of rare. Usually I sell these for 500 to 1,000 dollars.'

The price caused the boys to raise their eyebrows and the old man took notice.

'But I think I will close early today, so 100 dollars for the tooth and chain and 100 dollars for the box, how's that? offered the old man.

'Sold,' replied T-Rex, smiling at Hilton. Hilton was surprised the bidding was cut short by his friends' enthusiasm, but smiled and agreed.

'Deal,' said Hilton digging into his backpack for his wallet. The old man secured the tooth to a clasp and then used a sturdy leather shoe string so the tooth could be worn around Hilton's neck. The shop owner carefully tied the leather string around Hilton's neck and made sure the jagged tooth was clearly displayed. Hilton's two friends gave it the thumbs-up sign of approval.

'Never take it off,' said the old man. 'It will protect you day and night. That's just a little advice . . . free of charge of course.'

'Thanks,' said Hilton as the boys headed towards the exit.

'By the way, you may not know it yet, but today is the luckiest day of your life,' said the old man smiling.

The boys put on their sunglasses and walked down the street towards the restaurant.

'That old guy is either a fortune teller or a really good guesser,' stated Zack.

'This was almost the last day of my life,' remarked Hilton.

'No, he's right,' responded Zack, 'You're still alive. You could have drowned or even been killed out there today.'

'You're right Zack, maybe the old man knows something we don't,' replied Hilton.

T-Rex checked his watch. 'Past lunchtime! I'm starving . . . let's eat,' he exclaimed.

'We better hurry . . . he gets miserable when he's hungry,' joked Zack.

The café was just around the corner and the girls were probably feasting there already.

Down the street, two men, both wearing thick, black-framed sunglasses, stopped and examined a piece of paper. One man was short and fat with a bald patch in the middle of his head. His dress was sloppy, and he had the appearance of someone who was not very intelligent. The other man was very tall and extremely thin wearing a black fisherman's hat to protect himself from the sun and a very colourful flowered shirt. He moved clumsily, like he was about to tip over. The fat man pointed to the old man's shop and the skinny man nodded his approval. The two mysterious men walked directly to the storefront, stopped, looked around cautiously, opened the door, and went inside.

Chapter 3

INSIDE THE SHOP, the two men anxiously looked around at everything on the walls, the floor, hanging from the ceiling. They rummaged through the bins, discarding objects impatiently.

Hearing the commotion, the old man stepped through the doorway from the back room.

'Everything's for sale today,' the old man said in a friendly tone. 'Can I help you find something?'

'Chopstick, please tell this kind fellow what we require,' instructed the fat man.

'Right Fatty,' he replied. 'Sir, we believe you may be in possession of a certain article that may be of interest to us. Interested enough to buy it, if the price is right of course.'

'All my good stuff is back here, have a look, looking is free.'

The two men followed him into the musty back room. They began examining everything very carefully. They could not seem to find what they were looking for. They were puzzled.

'Can't see it here,' said Chopstick.

'What are you looking for? Maybe I know where it is,' replied the shopkeeper.

'Well, kind of like a telescope, really old, made of brass,' said Fatty.

The old man wiped the sweat from his forehead with a paper towel. What were the chances of two parties being after such an unusual item on the same day?

'I think it's called a spyglass,' added Chopstick.

'Remarkable,' the old man mumbled to himself. 'Well to be quite honest, I didn't even know I had one until that young man... uh well...stepped on it ...broke it... and bought it . . . today. That's the rule — you break it, you buy it. I still don't know where it came from. I thought I knew all by inventory pretty well . . . but . . . I had never seen that item before.'

'What boy?' asked Chopstick urgently.

'They left five minutes before you came in, three of them. Nice boys . . . very polite. They came in to buy a shark tooth. I made one of the boys kind of a good luck charm . . . so he could wear it around his neck.'

The two men quickly headed for the door. Chopstick pulled out his mobile phone and frantically pressed buttons. Once outside they quickly looked in all directions. They ran to the corner and looked up and down the narrow street. Chopstick stopped to talk on his phone.

'Yeah ... boss ... uh ... no, we didn't find it. But we know where it is ... well kind of...some kid has it ... apparently,' stuttered Chopstick.

'You bumbling idiots . . . find those kids . . . get my spyglass,' demanded the loud voice on the phone.

The angry man hung up and Chopstick looked at Fatty.

'Maybe they are still in the area,' said Fatty, 'Keep looking.'

'I told you we shouldn't have stopped for ice cream.'

Hilton, Cookie and their friends finished their soup noodles and headed for the minibus stop. The bus was just arriving, perfect timing. Fatty caught his breath and slapped Chopstick on the shoulder. From a long distance they saw a group of kids get into a minibus. Chopstick pointed and the two men rushed up the street, hoping to board the same bus. It was hopeless, they were too late.

'You think it was them?' asked Chopstick.

'I don't know, seemed to be a lot of them,' Fatty replied scratching his head. 'Where is this minibus going?'

The men looked at the bus-stop sign which indicated routes to Shatin.

'Looks like there are only two stops,' said Fatty. 'We'll take the next minibus and see where it takes us.'

Hilton and Cookie arrived home and unlocked the front door. Before going inside Hilton put his finger to his lips as a signal to Cookie not to say anything. Markus came running up to Hilton.

'Did you win? Did you win?' asked an excited Markus.

'Not this time partner,' replied Hilton.

Cookie ran into the living room looking for her parents.

'Hey everybody, Hilton almost got eaten by a shark, the biggest, meanest shark on earth,' she proclaimed loudly.

The sound of a plate smashing on the kitchen floor was heard by everyone. Their mother rushed from the kitchen and their father came out of his office upon hearing the outburst. Julien Chan was the chief criminologist for the Hong Kong Police Department, working out of the Central District office. He appeared very concerned.

Hilton gave Cookie a dirty look. She smiled innocently.

'Thanks for nothing,' he said in a quiet, angry voice.

'Are you all right, Hilton?' asked Robyn. Hilton shook his head, embarrassed at all the fuss.

'Son, are you sure you're okay?' asked Julien. 'You don't see too many sharks in Hong Kong and especially not in Stanley.'

'They're out there all right,' stated Grandpa Chan, as he made his way down from the top of the stairs.

'I don't even know if it was a shark,' replied Hilton defensively.

'Nobody else saw it, only me. Maybe it was just a shadow . . . a really big shadow . . . twice the length of my board, a shadow with spotty stripes, I don't know.'

'Tiger shark,' replied Grandpa quickly. They all looked at him, surprised.

'Pretty rare around here, but not impossible. They are real man-eaters. Most sharks attack you by mistake but not the tiger shark. It attacks you because he wants to eat you,' continued Grandpa. 'One bite and you're finished: 3,500 pounds of pressure per square inch. Enough to chop you right in half.'

Robyn gave her son a hug and went back into the kitchen to finish dinner. Julien gave his son a pat on the back and Grandpa grinned.

'Okay, okay, everyone just forget it. No big deal.

What kind of case are you working on Dad?' asked Hilton, changing the subject.

'Yeah dad,' interrupted Cookie. 'Tell us about it...please.'

'Well I can't say too much right now, but in a few days I'll be able to fill you in as much as I can. After all, police business is confidential,' replied Julien.

'Tell us more. I'm really interested, Dad,' said Hilton.

'Me too,' interjected Cookie, 'I like the stuff you do with the bugs.'

'Of course you two are interested. Probably want to follow in your father's footsteps, like I did. It is in the Chan blood,' continued Grandpa.

'I have a story to tell you kids, but wash up for dinner first.'

Hilton and Cookie sped up the stairs, showered quickly and met Grandpa in the living room. Markus tagged along as well, not wanting to miss any of the action. The kids loved to listen to Grandpa's stories. They were always different and very exciting. Not your usual boring tales.

Grandpa sat back comfortably in his chair and began: 'All you kids are interested police work and criminology because the Chans have been fighting crime for almost one hundred years. It all started with Great-grandfather Chan. He was the mayor of a farming village in Hunan province. The people there raised crops of wheat. It was harvest time and the men of the village used a hand-held farming tool called a scythe to cut the sheaves of wheat. This scythe was a two-foot long, razor-sharp steel blade fixed to a four-foot long wooden handle.

'Early one morning the village was awakened by a high pitched scream of horror. A woman walking through the wheat fields early one summer morning had discovered the bodies of a man and woman lying in a large pool of blood. They had been decapitated. There was no way to tell who these people were because the heads were missing. Who would do such a thing, and why?

'Great-grandfather concluded this was an act of passion and revenge. The blood had not dried, therefore the attack must have been committed only a short time ago. Grandfather knew the weapon used must be the scythe. It would be the only weapon available that could possibly inflict such a fatal injury. He summoned all the farmers to the centre of the village. He instructed all the men to step out into the middle of the street with their scythes. He walked slowly, stopping in front of each man, studying the blade of his scythe. On his initial pass, all appeared to be clean, no sign of blood. He stepped back and waited.

'The sun was bright and the midday heat was making everyone sweaty, but nobody dared to move. The men looked straight ahead offering no expression. No one professing their guilt. A few hours had passed and Grandfather began to take notice of one particular scythe. He waited for a few more minutes and then walked over and stood directly in front of one young man. "Why did you kill them?" he asked. The man hesitated and replied, "I did not kill anyone, sir." Grandfather then stated with firm authority, "Nature says otherwise."

'He then pointed to the blade of the scythe which

was now attracting a great number of flies. None of the other men's blades had any. Grandfather waited and the number of flies around the blade grew. The other villagers started to gather around. The villagers were amazed to see the flies swarming to the blade, though it appeared to be clean. The pressure became unbearable for the man and he soon broke down and confessed his guilt.'

The children smiled with approval at Great-grandfather's genius and clapped their hands.

'That's a great story,' commented Hilton.

'Wow Grandpa, you're the best,' affirmed Cookie.

'Why did the man kill those two people?' asked Hilton.

'The woman was to marry the man who committed the crime, but she loved another. That morning the murderer found them together and could not cope with the betrayal. A crime of passion and revenge,' stated Grandpa.

'Great-grandfather was pretty smart,' said Hilton.

'In those days there was no electron microscopes, DNA analysis, chemicals, or fingerprint dust,' replied Grandpa.

'Thank goodness we have them all today,' interrupted Julien Chan who had been listening in.

'Grandfather Chan was using entomology, the study of insects, to uncover the crime. He just called it "nature" because it is a natural occurrence. The blade was merely wiped clean, maybe washed with water. Not good enough to beat the keen sense of smell of the flies that were attracted to the seemingly invisible traces of blood on the murderer's blade.'

'Can you teach us more about the bugs, please

dad,' begged Cookie.

'Yeah dad this is really cool,' replied Hilton.

'I don't like bugs,' said Markus, 'I'm afraid.'

'You are a bug,' joked Cookie, and proceeded to tickle Markus.

'Time for dinner,' said Robyn, 'I'm not sure if anyone is very hungry after that.'

They all laughed and the children rushed to the table. Hilton told the family about his ordeal since Cookie had already spilled the beans. He showed them the shark-tooth necklace. He mentioned the brass spyglass and all the other cool things they'd seen at the shop. Cookie told them about Rico and his group of annoying friends. She also mentioned their shopping adventure in Stanley Market. They finished dinner and Hilton went up to his room while Cookie helped mom cleanup the dinner table and wash the dishes.

In his room Hilton looked around for a good place to put the glass case. His wall was full of movie posters, Bruce Lee, Jackie Chan, along with music posters, Edison, Out-Kast, and hundreds of CDs, mainly hip-hop artists from America. A boomerang hung on the wall, a souvenir he had brought back from Australia and one of his most prized possessions. His room was neater than most. Hilton hated a messy place. Markus came into the room and climbed up on a chair. Little brother took Hilton's model airplane and began pretending to fly it around the room. Hilton was busy looking for the right place to put his newest prize. He was not paying attention when Cookie burst in.

'Ice cream for everyone,' she said loudly, holding

two ice cream bars in her hands.

Markus jumped off the chair. In his excitement for ice cream, he stumbled into Hilton who tried to get out of the way and backed into Cookie. His hand holding the case bumped into his desk, dislodging the case from his hand. The small display box fell to the hardwood floor. The glass shattered on impact, releasing the spyglass from the antique enclosure.

Cookie and Markus stared at each other in disbelief. Everyone accused everyone else for the mishap. Julien appeared at the doorway. Everyone spoke at once, arguing their case. He motioned for everyone to stop and settle down.

'Cookie, please get a broom and the vacuum so we can clean this up,' he said calmly. 'You guys be careful, don't cut yourself.'

Hilton picked up the spyglass, checked it for damage, then showed it to his dad. Julien went to the window and looked through the spyglass. He extended it to its maximum length, about 40 centimetres He seemed puzzled, tried to look through both ends several times, then gave up.

'Can't see anything,' he said handing the spyglass back to Hilton.

Hilton went to the window and looked through it trying everything his dad did without success. Nothing but darkness. Hilton tried to gently extend it even further, turned the lens pieces as if focusing a camera, but nothing worked. He looked through it again as Cookie returned with the broom and dustpan.

'Thanks you two,' said Hilton. 'Looks like you guys broke it . . . it doesn't work at all, can't see anything.'

Cookie kept her head down and started sweeping the floor. A very quiet Markus nibbled innocently at his ice cream. Hilton was truly disappointed but continued trying to figure out why the spyglass did not work. He shook his head, showing his displeasure. Maybe something inside was broken or was blocking the lens. He played with the front lens to see if he could get it off. Finally, after a few minutes, Hilton was able to remove the front lens. Everyone moved in for a closer look.

Chapter 4

HILTON'S EYEBROWS BEGAN TO RISE as he cautiously peered inside the spyglass. He put his finger in the tube and slowly extracted a rolled-up silky, gold-coloured cloth. He took it over to his computer desk and carefully unrolled it. It was folded in three sections so he followed the folds and flattened it out. They all gathered around. What had Hilton found?

The thin shiny fabric measured about one metre wide by about one-and-a-half metres long. It covered the entire desk. On the front of the cloth was an ink drawing of a man's face, a very mean man by the look of his eyes. Hilton turned over the cloth and the other side revealed what looked like an old land map. There were some faded marks which might be Chinese writing. The three looked at each other and even Markus stuck his ice-cream-covered face in for a peek.

'Looks pretty cool,' said Cookie. 'What is it?'

Hilton shrugged. Julien picked the cloth up and tried to decipher the writing as he held it up to the light. He shook his head in a negative manner. Hilton put the lens back on the front of the spyglass. Cookie took it from his hand and went to the window. The boys continued to stare at the delicate cloth.

'It works now,' she said joyfully. 'I can see. . . . Wow, this really works.'

'Why don't you show this to Professor Chow,' suggested Julien, 'He might have a better idea what it is exactly. Maybe he can tell you if it is of any importance.'

'Good idea dad. Cookie and I will go tomorrow after school,' replied Hilton. 'Cookie, can you keep this secret, it could be valuable.'

Cookie acknowledged Hilton and crossed her heart as a sign of her promise to keep quiet this time. They cleaned up the broken glass and everyone got ready for bed.

Monday morning, Hilton and Cookie arrived at school, listening to hip-hop music on their MP3 players. There seemed to be a definite buzz in the air but the twins had no idea why.

Within minutes of entering the school yard, Hilton was surrounded by a large group of girls all wanting to hear the details of his brave escape. Both teens were overwhelmed by the reception, in fact quite speechless.

T-Rex and Zack came jogging over.

'Can you believe this?' said T-Rex to Hilton. 'That big-mouth Rico told the whole school this morning about how he beat you yesterday and the only excuse you could offer was this shark. He called it the "great, ghost shark", the shark nobody saw but you. What a jerk.'

Hilton was not really amused but managed a smile.

'You know what they say, there's no such thing as bad publicity,' replied Hilton looking over at a smiling and surprised Cookie.

'You never had this many girls wanting to talk to you before, eh Hilton?' said Zack laughing.

The school bell saved the day and all the students

headed for their individual classrooms. Hilton and Cookie knew this was going to be a day to remember. Without knowing it, Rico had launched Hilton into superhero status. His ploy to make Hilton appear as the sore loser of a windsurfing competition had backfired. It appeared Hilton was more popular than ever. Rico was nowhere to be found.

School ended and Hilton and Cookie were escorted by their close group of friends out the large front doors and off school property. Many students were still talking of Hilton's scary encounter. Exciting stories like this just don't happen every day. Hilton was already a very popular student, now Rico had turned Hilton into a school celebrity. Hilton took his fifteen minutes of fame in stride.

The group broke up so Hilton and Cookie could head for the University. They walked to the bus stop and waited.

'Every girl in school wanted to talk to you today,' said Cookie. 'Really have no idea why, can't see the attraction.'

'Yeah, what a stressful day. All that female attention wears a guy out, you know,' laughed Hilton.

'Even your classmate — what's her name — Rachel or something, she's kind of cute I guess, came by to speak with you.'

'I guess she's alright,' replied Hilton shyly.

Hilton would never admit to anyone, especially Cookie, that he thought Rachel was the prettiest girl in school. He liked her but until today she had never talked to him much other than to offer a passing hello.

'"I guess" . . . my foot,' replied Cookie. 'You like her, admit it. Before today she never even looked at you. Now all of a sudden you're the school's golden boy. Pulled off the great shark escape. Give me a break.'

'Here's our bus,' said Hilton. The two boarded and the bus left for the University.

Behind a clump of trees, far in the distance, Chopstick tapped Fatty on the shoulder and handed him the binoculars.

'Looks like we found our targets. The old man said they bought a shark tooth. Look what's around the kid's neck,' noted Chopstick proudly.

'Yeah, you're right, good eyes,' Fatty said sarcastically. 'Looks like we staked out the right area last night and got lucky. The boss should be happy.'

'They're getting on the bus,' said Chopstick. 'Let's see if we can follow them. Maybe they have the spyglass and we can convince them to sell it to us.'

'If that doesn't work, there's always the old-fashioned way of doing business with these brats,' replied Fatty. 'Law of the jungle — we just take it.'

About 20 minutes later Hilton and Cookie arrived at the campus and made a long trek, taking shortcuts through several buildings, finally arriving at the private office of Professor Jefferson Chow. They knocked and waited.

'Door is open, come on in.'

Professor Chow's office was a one-room library. The office walls were lined with thousands of reference books. His desk was littered with several open books, many files, and papers.

'Well, well, what a pleasant surprise,' said the professor looking up from his desk. He eased back in his chair, smiled and welcomed his guests.

Professor Chow taught English literature but also dabbled in local history. He was a tall man wearing a dark blue wool vest, a tan-coloured tweed sports jacket with navy-blue elbow patches and stylish reading glasses with half-moon lenses. His hair was getting a little grey on the sides and he liked to hold a pipe even though he had given up smoking years ago. The professor had attended secondary school with Julien Chan, where they became the best of friends and they still had lunch together from time to time.

'Hello professor, how are you?' the twins said together.

'Fine, just fine, busy as usual . . . but never to busy for my friends, how nice to see you two,' replied the professor. 'How's mom and dad, Markus? Come on, have seat, tell me what you two have been up to.'

Hilton and Cookie told the professor about the shark episode and the Stanley Market shop. After showing the professor his shark-tooth pendant, Hilton reached into his backpack and a brought out the spyglass.

'This is what we came to show you professor,' said Hilton unscrewing the front lens and carefully pulling out the silk cloth. 'We found this inside . . . just like this.'

Hilton handed the fabric to the professor who made some space on his desk top. He unravelled it gingerly and examined both sides. He looked closely at all the markings then retrieved a magnifying glass from his desk drawer. The professor examined it again, more closely this time. He sat back with a more serious look on his face. Hilton and Cookie waited for some response. Professor Chow seemed to be in deep thought, staring into space. He got up from his chair and went over to his wall of reference books. He took one from the shelf and went back to his desk. There he flipped through many pages before finding what he was looking for. Hilton and Cookie could only wait patiently for the professor to finish his research. He finally stopped on one page and turned the book around to Hilton and Cookie and pointed to a small picture at the top.

Hilton and Cookie leaned over and looked closely.

'Kind of looks like the man on the front side of the cloth,' suggested Hilton.

'But who is it professor?' asked Cookie.

'This man is a king from the Qing Dynasty,' replied the professor. 'The picture is not exactly the same and there is very little reference text for this picture. Most likely he is not the same person but I believe they are both from the same time and place. I will have to check into this further. I don't think the man on your silk cloth is a king. Look at his eyes, he looks very fierce. I have no idea who he is but I'll try my best to find out. The other side looks like a crude map of some kind.'

The professor turned over the cloth looking again at both the front and back. Hilton and Cookie looked at each other, hoping the professor would be able to solve the mystery right away.

'Don't get to excited, not just yet,' cautioned the professor. 'It may be nothing at all. Could be a fake, a children's toy, who knows, maybe meaningless . . . worthless.'

'But it may be real, right professor?' asked Hilton anxiously.

'Maybe, but the only way to tell how old this is, would be to do some tests on it,' commented the professor. 'Sort of like carbon-dating bones to see how old they are. If this cloth dates back a couple hundred years then you may really have something here. If you like, I'll have our department test it for you. Should have the results in a few days.' 'Yes please professor,' they said together. 'I sure hope it's real, we want to know for sure,' said Hilton. 'Leave it with me and I'll phone you when the tests have been completed. How's that?'

Hilton and Cookie found it difficult to hide their enthusiasm. They were jumping and dancing all the way down the long hallway, giving each other high fives.

Outside the building, the twins headed for the bus stop. They were unaware that they were being tracked from a distance. They were first in line at the bus stop and paid no attention to the two men who lined up a few people behind them. The men avoided any eye contact, trying to remain unnoticed. The twins boarded the bus and the two men walked past them and sat in the seat right behind them. Fatty pointed out the backpack as Hilton removed it, placing it on his lap. Chopstick nodded.

Hilton and Cookie were exhausted and hungry after the day's adventurers, and decided to stop for a bowl of soup noodles. After eating, they made their way to the KCR station and went to the end of the platform where there would be fewer people. Fatty and Chopstick slowly walked in their direction. Hilton glanced at the digital display informing them that the next train was due in one minute. Chopstick and Fatty positioned themselves directly behind the two teenagers. The crooks spotted the security camera and both pulled their hats down over their eyes. They were ready to make their move.

The announcement of the coming train blared over the PA system as the train pulled up and squealed to a full stop. The last car was empty. Hilton and Cookie were about to move forward when both Chopstick and Fatty quickly grabbed one strap near each of their shoulders. In a rough, pulling motion, they ripped the first strap free and then tried to tear the other from their arms. Hilton and Cookie were surprised but quick to defend. They each grabbed their remaining strap and spun the two attackers around. The young, athletic teens had excellent balance and startled the thieves with their quickness. Split-second reflex action allowed them to let go of their backpacks and kick the two assailants through the open doors into the train. They crashed into the wall on the opposite side of the car just as the train doors closed. The train moved away and Hilton and Cookie waved goodbye. The two thieves lay there stunned, clutching the two backpacks.

'Who were those idiots?' asked Cookie angrily.

'Guess we needed new backpacks anyways,' said Hilton calmly. 'You okay?'

'Of course,' replied Cookie. 'I told you Golden Dragon kung fu would come in handy one of these days.'

'Let's go make a report and get a taxi home,' said Hilton. 'These guys sure are lousy pickpockets.'

'They are going to retire very poor if they don't improve their technique,' joked Cookie. 'Oh well, no books . . . no homework tonight,' she laughed.

'Let's get going,' said Hilton. 'At least they didn't get my MP3 player. I just loaded it up with new music.

Chapter 5

HILTON AND COOKIE FOUND it very difficult to concentrate on their studies. They were anxiously awaiting the professor's call. What did the drawings mean? Who was the man in the picture? Why was the cloth in the spyglass? There were so many unanswered questions.

They realised that the tests would probably show the silk cloth to be recently made, merely placed inside the spyglass as some sort of joke. That was the reality, but they really hated to admit it.

They returned home from school feeling pretty worn out from the past days of excitement.

'Hilton, Cookie, is that you? There's a message for you,' Robyn called cheerfully.

They rushed into the kitchen. Both grabbed for the note affixed to the refrigerator with a pizza magnet, with Hilton beating Cookie to the punch. Hilton quickly picked up the phone and punched in the professor's number. The professor finally answered and Hilton began speaking in his usual polite manner. Cookie put her ear close to headpiece, straining to listen. The conversation was very short. Hilton thanked the professor and hung up. Hilton's face showed mixed emotions.

'Well?' asked Cookie excitedly.

'The good news is, the professor wants to see us after school tomorrow,' said Hilton looking puzzled. 'But he didn't sound too positive, so I have no idea what's going on.'

'You'll find out tomorrow,' answered Robyn. 'Don't take this so seriously.' 'No sleep again tonight,' announced Cookie.

Hilton agreed and they slowly dragged themselves upstairs to finish their homework.

The next day after school, Cookie and Hilton raced up the terraced stairways outside the University. Stopping in front of Professor Chow's office, they took a few deep breaths, nodded at each other, then Hilton knocked. The professor summoned them to enter.

'You made it,' said the professor smiling. He carefully laid out the silk cloth on his desk.

'Well kids, the tests prove this is approximately 200 years old,' proclaimed the professor. 'I admit I was quite surprised.'

The news caused Hilton and Cookie to freeze for a second, then they both began to smile. The professor continued.

'This portrait is of our most famous pirate, Cheung Po Tsai. The other side is some form of map. Probably something to do with Cheung Chau,' continued the professor as he turned the cloth over to the other side. 'That island was sometimes used as a base for his pirate fleet.'

'Wow,' said Cookie.

'Cheung Po Tsai?' asked Hilton. 'The name sounds a little familiar but I think we only learned a bit about him in school.'

'Well then, I guess it is time for a lesson in local history and folklore,' said the smiling professor.

Hilton and Cookie moved their chairs closer to the

professor's desk and began to listen intently.

'Two hundred years ago, pirates ruled the seas, waterways and islands around Hong Kong. The most famous of these pirates was Cheung Po Tsai. At his peak it is believed he controlled forty to sixty thousand pirate faithful and six to eight hundred ships. This vast armada dominated the Hong Kong waters, where they plundered ships at will.

'Cheung Po Tsai became a pirate quite unwillingly. At the age of fifteen, he was captured by Cheng Yat, the most powerful of the pirate chieftains. Cheng Yat recognised some leadership qualities in the young man. Soon Cheung Po Tsai was placed in charge of a fleet of pirate junks. He quickly became an anti-Qing rebel. A true pirate.

'In 1807, Cheng Yat was swallowed up by the sea during a ferocious storm. Under the guidance of his adopted mother Cheng Yi Soa, the wife of Cheng Yat, Cheung Po Tsai soon gained control of the entire Red Flag fleet.

'Cheng Yi Soa, also known as the 'Dragon Lady', soon fell in love with Cheung Po Tsai. They became a fearless team. Their domination of the waterways around Hong Kong was legendary. Many think she really ruled the formidable pirate fleet that defeated all the vessels of the Imperial Chinese navy sent to destroy them. They plundered Imperial vessels, stealing some of the emperor's most prized possessions. They controlled the coastal villages and used them as bases. But they could not remain in one place for too long. When villagers rose up against the pirates, the Dragon Lady ordered the villages burned to the ground and all the men killed. The women were never harmed, she demanded they be left untouched.

'Some legends depict Cheung Po Tsai as a kind of Robin Hood figure. He paid twice the market price for goods requisitioned from the coastal villages and treated foreign merchant ship with respect, only politely asking for protection money to pass through local waters. He founded coastal temples using their terraced landscapes as lookout points.

'The Qing Dynasty was becoming alarmed at the pirates' naval might and dispatched Viceroy Pai Ling to the region. Trade with the pirates was now forbidden and Chinese merchant ships were banned from the area. The pirates began to attack foreign ships which raised the anger of the British and Portuguese governments. The Portuguese decided to align with the British and Chinese fleets to form a blockade of the Lantau Channel, the centre of Cheung Po Tsai's operations. Cheung negotiated the assistance of a rival pirate leader, commander of the Black Flag fleet. They prepared for battle.

'But when the time came, the Black Flag fleet was not there to bolster Cheung's position. Cheung Po Tsai and the Dragon Lady were alone to fight the British, Portuguese, and Chinese fleets. The historic battle lasted for nine days with Cheung Po Tsai victorious. He vowed vengeance on the leader of the Black Flag fleet for his betrayal. The Black Flag pirates soon defected to the Chinese government, who granted them amnesty.

'In 1810 it was quite evident the pirate days for Cheung Po Tsai and the Dragon Lady were coming to an end. They could not continually battle with these nations whose fleets were becoming larger and more dedicated to their demise. The pirate king and queen negotiated a surrender of their 200-plus junks and more than 17,000 pirates.

'For a short time Cheung Po Tsai assisted the Chinese government by capturing many of the remaining pirates. He was declared a class three Imperial official, retiring to a piece of land on Hong Kong Island. The Dragon Lady went to Canton where she operated a gambling house and died at the age of 60.

'Where all the treasure he collected over the years is, nobody knows. It is possible it is still buried or hidden out there somewhere. It is also possible Cheung Po Tsai returned all the stolen treasure back to the government in exchange for his life of freedom.'

The professor's story was finished and he stood up to stretch. Hilton and Cookie relaxed back in their chairs, looked at each other and smiled. They were impressed and starting to feel very proud of themselves.

'That was a great story professor,' commented Cookie. Hilton nodded in agreement.

'Most of it is probably true,' injected the professor. 'One thing is for sure, this banner is real and is probably worth some money to a collector or museum.' The two straightened up in their chairs, eyes wide open and gleaming, as they clapped their hands with quiet approval.

'The writing on the back I left alone because I did not want to take any chances of damaging the cloth,' said the professor. 'Maybe your father has a more gentle method of clarifying the writing and markings on the other side.'

The professor rolled up the cloth, placed it back in the spyglass and handed it to Hilton who placed in a waist pouch. Hilton and Cookie shook the professor's hand and thanked him numerous times for his assistance. Hopefully Dad could help decipher the faded hand writing and enhance the image of what looked like a map on the opposite side of the pirate flag. Hilton and Cookie never said it, but they were sure this was no ordinary map. This had to be a real treasure map. A real pirate treasure map indeed. The treasure map of Cheung Po Tsai.

Chapter 6

COOKIE AND HILTON ARRIVED HOME, still bubbling over with excitement and wanted to tell everyone the amazing news immediately!

They gathered the family into the living room and began to relate the story of the Hong Kong pirates in every detail. Hilton took out the silk cloth and the family looked at it with amazement. Cookie turned it over, revealing the faded map outline and antique script. She explained that the professor had no real idea what it all meant. The script appeared to be Chinese characters, but quite unclear. Julien took the flag and held the flag up to the light and studied the structure.

He stood up, flag in hand, and began walking in the direction of his small home-office and makeshift laboratory.

'Hilton, Cookie, come with me, I have an idea,' said Julien.

Usually the children were not allowed in this room. Today was an exception. They followed their father into the room with its window overlooking the Shatin Racecourse where Julien worked in seclusion on many of his important police cases. Julien sat down at the elongated table and reached for a jar.

'Hopefully this powder will fill in pores of cloth around the writing and drawing,' said Julien, as he lightly sprinkled the powder onto the fabric 'It won't harm the material and we can easily shake it out later.'

Under normal lighting there appeared to be no change. Julien dimmed the lights and picked up an unusual torch.

'This ultra-violet light will cause the powder to fluoresce,' explained Julien. 'Watch.'

Julien had Cookie turn off the room light completely. Turning on the 'black light' he slowly moved it over writings on the cloth. Hilton and Cookie were captivated by what they saw. The outline of the map glowed in the dark and the image was much clearer. The script had also been enhanced enough to make out some of the characters.

'That's better,' said Julien confidently. 'I'll get the digital camera and we'll take a picture of the flag under the black light. Then you can bring it up on your computer monitor and see if you can figure anything out.'

Julien took the camera and snapped several pictures of the flag.

'There, that should do it guys,' said Julien. Cookie brought the room lighting back to normal. Julien tenderly patted out the dust from the flag and handed the flag back to Hilton.

'You two don't get caught up in all these notions of pirate treasure,' cautioned Julien. 'Most of these tales are untrue and most of the so called treasure was found a long time ago. Just have fun with it. Don't let this interfere with your school work.'

Outside their home, a car was parked on the opposite side of the street. Two dark figures sat inside patiently waiting for the house lights to go out. Chopstick and Fatty were waiting in the shadows.

'My hip is still sore from where they kicked me,'

complained Chopstick in a quiet, angry tone.

'Yeah . . . my neck still hurts,' replied Fatty. 'Payback time is coming soon.'

Hilton and Cookie transferred the camera image to their computer. They stared at the screen for over an hour, discussing the possibilities of what the script might say. It was getting late. They decided to take a print out to the Central Library to see if they could find any kind of corresponding information. Tomorrow could not come soon enough. Lights out, time to go to sleep.

The two thugs watched as all the house lights went out. They waited 30 minutes and made their move. They climbed over the small, decorative wall surrounding the property and started towards the house. They tip-toed with care over the soft carpet of grass, not making a sound . . . until they tripped the motion detectors and were met with the bright flash of outdoor spotlights. The entire front of the house was illuminated. At the same time the automatic lawn sprinkler system came on, drenching the two intruders with water.

Soon the whole neighbourhood would be able to see them. They had to make a run for it. In their haste to retreat back to the safety of the shadows, they slipped and stumbled on the damp lawn. Helping each other maintain their balance, they scrambled onto the brick pathway leading to the front gate. They crawled over the wall and hurried back to the car and crouched down, out of sight. Julien opened the front door to check on the disturbance. He stood there until the security lights went out, sending the yard back into darkness.

'Must have been the neighbour's cat,' mumbled Julien as he went back inside.

The two bumbling thieves came up from the floorboards of their old vehicle, still startled and soaking wet.

'Let's get out of here,' said Chopstick nervously. 'We'll get them tomorrow.'

'I am really starting to hate these kids,' replied Fatty.

They started the car and drove off.

The next day, Hilton and Cookie arrived at the Central Library in Causeway Bay, eager to find clues to reveal the secret of the pirate's flag.

They concentrated on the map outline. The most obvious place to start was Cheung Chau. After all, that is where Cheung Po Tsai had his legendary cave, the reported hiding place for his vast treasure. They retrieved several books with maps of the island today, as well as what it looked like some 200 years ago. Since the map outline on the flag was incomplete, Hilton tried to match up sections with their picture printout. Cookie kept bringing the reference material over to their table and Hilton continued searching for a match. Finally, Hilton thought he had something.

'Cookie . . . look,' Hilton whispered with mild excitement.

Cookie leaned over as Hilton pointed to a part of the picture that closely resembled a section of shoreline in the book.

'That's it,' confirmed Hilton. 'Now we know for

sure that this map has something to do with Cheung Chau. Maybe the treasure is still there, buried somewhere, hidden. Who knows?'

'Now we just have to try and figure out what these Chinese characters or symbols mean,' added Hilton. 'Then we would really have a good idea of what we are dealing with. Let's start with the ones that a fairly clear and see if we can fill in the blanks.'

The two sleuths began by copying the fragmented characters from the flag, onto a piece of paper to see if they could make any sense of them. Some were clearer than others and they wrote down northeast and northwest. That was about all they could be certain of. Not much to go on. Anything more would be a pure guess. There appeared to be several short lines of text and then what looked like a partial signature. They were certain it was the signature of Cheung Po Tsai, however they could not find any books in the library which displayed such a marking. The short lines of faded and broken Chinese characters were much clearer on their computer picture than on the original flag fabric. That was a great help. Unfortunately this writing was very foreign to them. Maybe the pirates had their own set of symbols, some kind of code. Hilton and Cookie would ask their father if they were on the right track and if there was any possible way of decoding the text. They packed up and left the library.

A stream of tram cars passed by and on the other side of the busy street Fatty and Chopstick were watching the teenagers closely from the cover of traffic. The crooks could not believe their good fortune when Hilton and Cookie crossed the street, a mere 30 metres ahead of them. The teens stopped at the mid-street platform and boarded the very next tram. The two hoodlums focused on their targets and quickly jumped onto the same car. They pulled their caps down, looking up from time to time, making sure the two youths did not make an unexpected departure. As the tram headed into Wan Chai the two men tried to sneak a little closer, but the tram slowed, stopped, and Hilton and Cookie quickly jumped off. Fatty and Chopstick were caught off-guard but hopped off as well. The two men were gaining position, just about to pounce, when Hilton and Cookie took a few quick steps, a quick right turn, and rushed into a large building.

The two pursuers adjusted their caps to get a better view then stopped and looked up at the sign on the building: ARSENAL HOUSE POLICE HEADQUARTERS.

They turned, lowered their heads and walked away very quickly in opposite directions.

The twins' appearance was a pleasant surprise for Julien as he came out to meet them in the lobby. He was very impressed with their research and agreed to help them try and decipher the old Chinese characters on the map. Julien could not guarantee success but would check the police language data base in search of answers. Hilton gave his dad their computer printout and he took it back inside the secured area of the police station.

In a few days the final windsurfing competition of the season would be held on Cheung Chau. Hilton decided he had to get in some practice and sharpen his skills. There was no way he was going to let Rico Wong beat him this time.

The next day was Buddha's birthday, a public holiday. They would go to the beach where Hilton could practice. Cookie decided to organise a beach barbecue which would include their close friends and schoolmates.

The twins entered the MTR station in Wan Chai, and headed for home. The carriage was very crowded and they had to stand. During the entire trip, Cookie felt like someone was watching her. They transferred to the KCR line at Kowloon Tong but her feeling did not change. She kept looking from side to side, forward and behind, trying to see over the heads on the crowded rail car. She felt very uneasy. Something just did not feel right.

Chapter 7

THE NEXT DAY, Hilton and Cookie were the first to arrive at Repulse Bay for the beach party. Cookie was weighed down with a large picnic basket filled with food for the barbecue. Hilton dragged his sailboard in the sand and followed Cookie to the designated spot. He helped Cookie unload the food and drinks onto the picnic table and then headed for the water. Hilton guided the board out into deeper water, looking down into the blue ocean constantly for any sign of uninvited guests.

The rest of their friends arrived shortly after, bringing more drinks, snacks, chips, and desserts. Echo, Sammie, T-Rex, and Zack were joined by two other schoolmates, Carson, a chubby type who was a mathematical wiz, and Ashley, a small-framed, pretty girl with colourful hair and bubbly personality.

Hilton was already far off shore, practising his tricks and techniques. The group on the beach all looked out at Hilton and waved. He responded by giving a surfer's 'hang ten' signal.

'Hilton looks good out there today,' commented T-Rex. 'This Sunday is the big challenge. That idiot Rico will learn a lesson, a lesson he'll never forget.'

'Come on you guys, don't just stand there admiring Hilton, help us out,' said Sammie.

'Better get to work boys, the girls must be hungry,' laughed Zack.

A car pulled up near the beach, slowed and finally

parked. Inside sat Fatty and Chopstick. They spotted the group of teens, got out of the car, and opened the trunk. They took out their towels, beach umbrella, and beach chairs, and slowly made their way in the direction of the teenagers. They placed their stuff on the sand about fifteen metres away from the barbecue pit and got comfortable.

'There's too many of them,' whispered Chopstick as he set up the chairs.

'Just watch and listen. See if we have an opportunity to get those two kids away from the group, relax will you,' replied Fatty.

They strained to hear the conversations and eyed Hilton as he beached his sailboard and arrived on the scene.

'I'm starving,' said Hilton, as he shook the water from his head onto the girls.

'Whoops,' he said, laughing and running away from their mean stares.

'Hilton . . . if you want to eat, start cooking,' said Cookie. 'And cook lots, everyone is hungry, not just you.'

'Come on guys let's show these girls who the real chefs are,' said Hilton patting his male counterparts on the shoulder as a signal to help him barbecue the pork chops and chicken wings.

The friends spent the entire afternoon eating, joking, swimming, and consuming a large amount of soft drinks, until finally the hot sun took its toll and it was time to pack up and head for home.

The group disposed of all the rubbish and Cookie made sure everyone placed all the cans and plastic containers in the proper rubbish and recycle bins.

Hilton gave a last look behind to make sure they had taken all their personal belongings from the barbecue area. They began to leave.

Fatty and Chopstick stood up, frustrated and sunburned.

'So the little monsters are going to Cheung Chau this weekend,' commented Fatty.

'Yeah, some stupid windsurfing contest,' replied Chopstick. 'I think they said Sunday.'

'Good, they won't be hard to find,' said Fatty. 'Let's tell the boss. We'll follow them just in case we can get them alone.'

'You look funny,' laughed Chopstick pointing at Fatty's sunburned face.

'You look stupid,' replied Fatty. 'Normal for you.'

The two crooks went back to their car. The girls boarded the minibus and Hilton waited with the guys for Zack's older brother to show up with his jeep. The vehicle would accommodate Hilton's sailboard if they stood it straight up. The jeep was pretty crowded when the boys left the beach-front area but everyone was used to that.

Hilton, seated at the back, noticed two men sporting sunglasses driving behind the jeep. He didn't think too much about it, and relaxed and enjoyed the breeze from the jeep's open-air ride.

The ocean breeze combined with the sun and all the day's activities had succeeded in almost putting the passengers to sleep. Their drowsiness was interrupted when the jeep came to a screeching halt. All the boys jumped up, now wide awake.

'What's going on?' asked Hilton removing his mirrored sunglasses and rubbing his eyes.

'Accident,' said Zack pointing directly ahead. 'Just happened.'

Hilton quickly jumped from the car. 'Let's see if we can help,' he said. 'Come on guys, let's go.' All the boys jumped from the jeep and ran up to the scene of the accident to see if anyone was hurt. Hilton gave T-Rex his mobile phone.

'Call 999,' said Hilton as he and the others looked into the vehicles and asked if everyone was all right.

The boys were busy with the accident victims and now sirens could be heard in the distance. Hilton looked back to see when the ambulance would arrive and caught a glimpse of two men close to the jeep. He thought he saw one of them reach into it. The sirens stopped as the medical teams arrived.

'Who are those two guys?' asked Hilton loudly. 'There, at the jeep, let's go!'

The others jumped alertly and they all started running back towards the jeep.

Fatty startled Chopstick with a slap on the arm, pointing to the five teenagers running back towards them. The two crooks quickly ran to their car, jumped in, made a U-turn and drove off speedily.

'After them,' yelled Hilton as they all piled into the jeep.

The jeep backed up and was about to turn when one of the ambulances slowly moved forward, blocking their attempt. They were stuck.

Fatty and Chopstick continuously looked back, checking the rear view and side mirrors, their hearts racing. They saw the traffic jam behind with not a single car able to follow, and knew their escape had been successful.

Hilton finally arrived home and was met by Cookie. Where have you been?' she asked.

'There was a car accident and we got caught in the traffic jam,' replied Hilton.

Cookie looked at Hilton's facial expression. She could always tell when something was wrong or he had something important on is mind.

'What else . . . let's have it,' she demanded.

Hilton knew she would keep asking until he told her.

'Two guys tried to steal our backpacks from the jeep while we were helping the people involved in the car accident,' replied Hilton.

'You're kidding,' said Cookie quite surprised.

'I think they were the same guys who tried to rob us at the KCR station,' continued Hilton. 'I'm not sure, they were quite far away, one was short and fat and the other slim and tall.'

Cookie raised her eyebrows. 'Why would they be interested in us?'

'This all started shortly after we found the spyglass,' said Hilton.

'Exactly,' replied Cookie. 'We've got a real mystery on our hands now, don't we?'

'We'll ask dad if he has any news for us on the Chinese characters when he gets home tonight.'

Cookie nodded and they went upstairs to finish their homework assignments for tomorrow.

Julien Chan came home just as dinner was finishing. Robyn cleared the table and set a place for Julien. The twins could hear their father's voice and appeared in the room to greet him.

'Homework all done?' asked Julien.

'Come on dad, did you find out anything?' the twins asked together anxiously.

'As a matter of fact, I did,' Julien replied. 'Let's go into my office.'

'It does not seem to make a lot of sense,' began Julien. 'Maybe only to the writer, possibly our pirate friend, Cheung Po Tsai. Looks like his signature and those Chinese characters mention the directions northwest and northeast, and makes reference to the "king of beasts". I don't know if it's a poem, a riddle, a message, or a clue. Very difficult to understand . . . I'll read it for you:

> '*King of beasts ... protect ... sign ...*
> *calculate proper line*
> This part is very faded ...
> *Do not go here... stay away ...*
> Some kind of faded symbol ...
> *Northeast or northwest*
> *Wind is best*
> *Three boxes rest*
> Looks like it is signed ... this area is faded, then ... *Po Tsai.*

'This style of writing is old, perhaps 300 years pd according to our experts at the station,' said Julien.

'That's great dad . . . thanks,' said Hilton smiling. 'At least we have something to work with now.'

'Just think if we can solve this mystery, we'll be famous,' said Cookie excitedly.

'Don't get carried away,' cautioned Julien. 'When

you go to Cheung Chau this weekend just have fun. The competition is Sunday, concentrate on that first.'

'Dad . . . would it be all right if Cookie and I go over Saturday morning . . . uh so I can practise?' asked Hilton. Cookie went over and hugged her father while nodding her approval.

'We can stay with Uncle 6 . . . he has a place there,' said Cookie. 'Please dad . . . please, please, pleassssse.'

Julien looked at his two children. He knew what they were up to, but agreed.

The twins had started upstairs when Julien turned to them.

'And you two, don't go digging up the whole island,' said Julien 'Digging on government land is illegal. Don't get yourselves into any trouble.'

'Trouble . . . us?' replied Cookie looking at Hilton. They both looked at their father innocently. Julien shook his head, smiling.

In Hilton's room they wrote out everything their father had told them, word for word. They brought up the picture on the computer screen and tried to visualise what Cheung Po Tsai had meant.

The next two days felt like ten. Friday night was mostly sleepless, full of anticipation. Could they crack the pirate's code?

Unravel the code and solve the mystery. The pirate's treasure would be the ultimate reward. If they found the secret hiding place would the treasure still be there? They could only dream and hope for now. At this point there were so many questions and very few answers.

Saturday morning finally arrived. Wake up —
time to go to work.

Chapter 8

THE TWINS WERE UP at the crack of dawn, loading their backpacks with necessities for their overnight stay. Hilton brought along a few prized possessions like his lucky Australian boomerang and his new spyglass. The pirate's flag was carefully folded and placed in a Ziploc bag concealed in a money sack secured around his waist. They also assembled a small tool kit, first-aid supplies, rope, compass, pens, pencils, paper, and two large flashlights.

Their mother had prepared a nourishing breakfast which the two teenagers gobbled down quickly. Everyone said goodbye and Hilton and Cookie followed their father out to the car. The twins should have been tired from their lack of sleep but the thought of a pirate treasure hunt was the only fuel they needed to keep their spirits high and energy level at maximum. It was about a 30-minute drive and finally they had arrived at the Outlying Islands Pier in Central. Julien pulled up to the curb and stopped. The twins couldn't get out fast enough.

'Now, Uncle 6 should be there to meet you, so don't leave the pier area without him,' instructed Julien. 'Don't give your uncle a hard time and stay out of trouble.'

'You know us dad, we're no trouble,' joked Cookie. 'Hilton — promise dad you won't cause any problems.'

'I know you, I know you both very, very well,'

replied a smiling Julien. 'Be good, and have fun.'

The ferry left the pier, estimated time of arrival: 55 minutes. The vessel chugged its way out of Victoria Harbour, and the first 30 minutes seemed an eternity for the restless pair. Finally they spotted the small, hilly piece of land coming up on the right side of the ferry. Cookie slapped Hilton on the shoulder, drawing his attention to her line of sight. As they neared Cheung Chau they both observed the coastline carefully. Hilton took out his spyglass and noted the small coves, bays, and brush covered hillsides. He tried to imagine possible hiding places for the pirate's treasure. Where would he hide a great treasure if he were the Prince of Pirates?

They tried to imagine themselves as pirates two centuries ago. The options looked endless as the ferry passed the treed landscape, many small inlets, and rocky terrain.

The ferry steamed around the typhoon shelter and headed into port, docking at the ferry terminal.

It was still early morning as they quickly walked off the ferry and looked around for Uncle 6. Several metres away a slender man moved in their direction, waving and smiling. It was Uncle 6. They greeted each other and all walked back to their uncle's flat.

'Cookie, Hilton, good to see you again,' said Uncle 6. 'Relax for awhile. There are drinks and food in the fridge. Then when you're ready, the island awaits you.'

'We are going to do a little exploring this afternoon,' explained Hilton.

'I know you have a competition tomorrow at Tung Wan Beach,' said Uncle 6. 'I'll join the rest of your family to cheer you on.'

'Thanks Uncle 6,' replied Hilton.

'I'll leave you two alone to enjoy the island,' said Uncle 6. 'If you need anything, just phone me, I have some things to attend to. You can't get lost, just be careful if you're out near the water, and don't go to close to the edge of the cliffs.'

They agreed to be careful and Uncle 6 left to run his errands.

Hilton and Cookie put a couple boxes of ice-cold lemon tea in their backpacks and were ready to go. Their first call: Cheung Po Tsai's cave.

They walked back to the pier and began to follow the harbour shoreline. They walked slowly, noting everything around them. The harbour was the home to hundreds of sampans and small junks. Tourists and locals whizzed by on bicycles and small motorised wagons. The island was void of automobiles, no cars permitted. At the road's end they began their ascent along a pathway up the hillside. It was not long before they arrived near the summit, rounded the corner and made their way to the mouth of the cave.

The entrance to the cave was surprisingly small, a mere slit in the side of a great rock wall. They made their way to the opening and looked inside. It was dark and uninviting. Hilton and Cookie thought Cheung Po Tsai and his men must have been very slim as a large or tall man would have little chance of fitting through the narrow opening. They looked at each other . . . time to check it out.

'You first older brother, age before beauty,' laughed Cookie.

70

'Go ahead, be the first to find the treasure, I insist,' replied Hilton.

'You're the brave one,' Cookie urged. 'C'mon it's getting hot out here.'

Hilton knew she wouldn't move, he had no choice.

'You're a real baby you know,' said Hilton as he stepped down a three-rung steel ladder and into the mouth of the cave. 'Follow me.'

The interior of the cave was pitch black. They switched on their flashlights and inched their way forward. It was even difficult to see with their lights on. Hilton quickly turned to Cookie.

'Boo!,' he said sharply.

Cookie jumped.

'Scared yet?' asked Hilton.

'Very funny, ha . . . ha . . . ha . . . Mister Funny Man,' replied Cookie. 'Hope you see a ghost . . . hope he scares the crap out of you,' she whispered.

Proceeding slowly, they illuminated the walls and ceiling of the cave searching for some mark, a sign, or a clue, something somebody had missed in the past. The interior of the cave was cool and wet. The footing was very uneven, causing their balance to give way on several occasions. They had to brace against the damp walls as they moved forward. They came to an area where the cave widened and they could stand upright and pause to have a better look around. They went up and down every inch of the walls, floor, and ceiling. Finding nothing of interest, they continued forward. The cave narrowed again and they came to another steel ladder which they led them up and out a second hidden exit. They climbed up a few rocks to the cement pathway leading back to the original starting point. The twins were very disappointed. It seemed the 'Legendary Cheung Po Tsai Cave' was just a ploy to attract tourists.

'They must be kidding,' proclaimed Cookie. 'There's no treasure in there, that's for sure.'

'It's kind of like a small vault,' replied Hilton scratching his head. 'This sure isn't what I expected.'

They sat on a large rock for awhile, with a definite feeling of disappointment. Hilton stood up and took out his spyglass. He proceeded outside the metal guardrail to get a good look at the surrounding area. Eastward, across a small bay, looked like a perfect landing area. Cheung Po Tsai's cave had no such place where a ship might dock. The cave's entrance could only be accessed by climbing up a steep and jagged cliff face. Lifting heavy chests filled with treasure would be quite a burden for even the strongest of pirates. But maybe that's why Cheung Po Tsai had liked the location. It was not visible from the sea and difficult to get to.

Hilton observed the surf crashing against the huge boulders below. He pointed out to Cookie what looked like a small opening in the rocks below. Could it be another cave entrance? One that would surely be hidden by the waterline when the tide was in.

'Cookie, let's go through the cave one more time, double-check every square inch,' said Hilton. 'Then we'll make our way down there and check out that opening.'

'This can't be all there is,' moaned Cookie. 'We must have missed something . . . some small thing that only a trained eye could spot. I will really concentrate this time.'

They climbed back into the cave. The examination of the cave's interior became intense. Inch by inch, the beams from the flashlights slowly passed over the damp walls, rocky floor, and stained ceiling. Hilton led the way with Cookie covering his tracks two metres behind.

Cookie was focused, deep in thought when she caught a glimpse of something out of the corner of her eye. She shook her head and stared forward. She concentrated the light on a spot near the ceiling of the cave. She stopped in her tracks. A stream of air seemed to pass right through her. So cold, it made shivers run down her spine. Her eyes began to water and she looked up into the light. Her jaw dropped.

Before her eyes appeared a menacing figure, it could only be the Prince of Pirates, the ghost of Cheung Po Tsai. There he stood in all his glory. His cold stare seemed to hypnotise Cookie, and she felt paralysed for the moment. She could not move or speak. The apparition's right eye was covered with a black narrow patch and a long scar ran from the corner of his eye down the side of his cheek. He was youthful in appearance, unshaven, with shoulder-length hair that was unkempt, tangled, and filthy, in contrast with his braided goatee held together at the bottom with a cross of gold. He wore a black head scarf with a red skull insignia, knotted, with a tail hanging down the left side of his head, The remainder of his unflattering ensemble included baggy black trousers, tattered leather boots, and a battle-worn yellow silk jacket open from his neck to his waist exposing a tanned chest and a tattoo over his heart. The tattoo of a crimson skull. In his left hand he held a flintlock pistol and the right brandished a gleaming, blood-stained cutlass. The ghostly buccaneer did not speak, only looked to the right and motioned with his sword.

Cookie stood still, quiet as a church mouse. She wanted to scream but could not manage a sound. She tried to call out to Hilton, warn him, alert him, but nothing came out. She tried to run but her muscles would not move. The ghost turned his cruel gaze upon her. With sword in hand, he rubbed the skull tattoo with his fist and extended the cutlass through the wall of the cave. Cookie thought she saw the blade pass through three treasure chests floating in mid air. She told herself this must be a mirage and closed her eyes quickly to refocus. Regaining some courage, she slowly opened her eyes not knowing what to expect. The pirate brought his cutlass back into full sight and held it high above his head. Suddenly a new terror invaded Cookie's mind as the left side of the ghost pirate's face began to melt away. Like a burning candle dripping its hot wax, the flesh and blood began to liquefy, exposing the bones, broken teeth, and a large, ominous, empty eye socket. Cookie was in shock, frightened beyond words, and certain this merciless ghost was about to deliver a blow that would surely decapitate her. She thought she saw the ghost motion the weapon downward in her direction. She closed her eyes tightly, braced herself, and prepared for the impact of the razor-sharp steel. As she stood in eerie silence, it was impossible to remove the image of the fierce pirate from her mind. Cookie sensed her time had come. It would be all over in a split second. There was nothing she could do to stop it.

A few seconds passed in the cool stillness and she felt nothing. A wave of frosty air blew through her hair. Some warmth returned to the cave and she slowly opened her eyes. The ghost was gone.

She looked around, up, down, and behind her, taking no chances, the ghost might still be watching. Her heart pounding and knees weak, she struggled to catch up with Hilton. He had already reached the exit ladder. She grabbed him from behind. Hilton flashed the light in her eyes.

'What . . . what's the matter?' asked Hilton.

She babbled for several seconds and Hilton could not understand a single word.

'Did you see it . . . did you see it, Hilton?' continued a frightened Cookie.

'See what?' replied Hilton. 'What's the matter with you all of a sudden? I think you need some fresh air. You look like you've seen a ghost.'

'Cheung Po Tsai . . . I saw him . . . right back there, waving and pointing,' she replied motioning in the direction of the sighting.

Hilton stepped around Cookie and took a few steps back into the cave. He positioned his flashlight and looked for a while, then shook his head.

'Nothing there little sister,' he replied. 'It was probably just a shadow or something. Relax.'

'Really, he was there,' she stuttered. 'Now I know what he looks like . . . really scary with a big red birthmark or some weird blotch on his chest. Oh yeah, and a big black eye patch over his right eye. I thought he was going to kill me with his sword. Waving it everywhere . . . put it right through the cave wall. I closed my eyes when I thought he was going to chop my head off . . . then he just disappeared.'

'Should have called me, I was right there,' proclaimed Hilton.

'I tried, really I did,' she replied. 'But no sound came out.'

'That's a first,' said Hilton laughing. 'Impossible, no way. You, no sound? I don't think so.'

Cookie punched him in the arm for his untimely remark and pushed by him in disgust.

'Let's settle down and go explore that other cave below,' directed Hilton. 'Take a few deep breaths and you'll be okay.'

Several minutes later they emerged from the cave again. Cookie could not get the image of Cheung Po Tsai out of her mind. The teens took a few moments to adjust to the sunlight, then slowly began making their way to the shoreline below.

'I know you don't believe me, but I saw him,' said Cookie. 'He stared at me and his face started melting . . . it was so gross . . . super scary.'

'I believe you,' replied Hilton in a patronising tone. 'I just wish he could have told you where the treasure was hidden instead of scaring you half to death.' Hilton turned away and laughed as he continued downward. They navigated the rocks very carefully. One wrong move could spell disaster.

They moved slowly over the rocks and Cookie slipped, grabbing Hilton abruptly. He guided her down and they reached the opening, but it was not an entrance to a second cave, just a shallow recess. There was nothing here to see. They made their way back to the summit, disappointed the caves had not yielded a single clue.

Hilton looked around to make sure they were alone and then brought out the printout of the map. They were certain the key to finding the treasure was hidden in this picture. They knew it was there somewhere … but where? Perhaps something on the island would provide a clue to the riddle.

They made their way back towards the pier, and decided to rent bicycles. This way they could travel faster and Hilton could conserve some energy for tomorrow's big test.

They visited the graveyard, heard stories of the bun festival, and rode up to a lookout pavilion which provided a panoramic view of Tung Wan Beach from the opposite end of the island. They finally found their way to Pak Tai Temple. The temple was built in 1783 and dedicated to the 'Supreme Emperor of the Dark Heaven'. Inside they found a sword reported to be over 1,000 years old, found by fishermen. They both admired the intriguing relic. The statues of two fierce generals, Thousand Miles Eye and Favourable Wind Ear stood by the altar. They had the power to hear and see everything. They probably knew where the treasure was but they weren't telling anyone.

'I sure wish I had their power,' said Hilton starring at the statues.' Be real handy right about now.'

'You're not kidding,' replied Cookie as they both walked outside and sat on the temple stairs.

There was silence for several minutes, as they took a break, managing a few long sips of their lemon tea. Hilton and Cookie could hear the voices of children, birds singing, and the clicking sound of the local islanders playing mah-jong somewhere in the distance. Hilton stood up to stretch and loosen his neck muscles. Suddenly, something caught his attention. He walked towards the two lion statues guarding the entrance to the temple.

'Hilton, you know what I think . . .' began Cookie. She looked up to see Hilton heading for the statues.

She jumped up to join him, sensing something had caught his interest.

'Cookie, remember what dad said about the text? Something about the "king of beasts"?' asked Hilton.

'I remember. So?' replied Cookie.

Hilton looked at Cookie and spoke in a serious tone, 'The lion is the king of beasts.'

They both looked at each other.

'Look what we have here,' added Hilton grinning.

'Maybe the lions, guardians of the temple, are also guardians of the treasure,' said Hilton.

Chapter 9

HILTON STUDIED THE STONE LION, starting at the base and working his way from back to front. Cookie tried to follow his lead.

'What exactly are you looking for?' asked Cookie.

'I don't really know,' replied Hilton. 'Something out of the ordinary, something that shouldn't be there. This temple was built before Cheung Po Tsai was born. My guess is the lions were here as well.'

'You check out this one and I'll start looking at the other lion, then we'll switch so we can double check,' suggested Cookie.

Hilton nodded and continued. He grabbed a magnifying glass from his backpack and took a closer look, studying every inch of the lion. The bright afternoon sun made it difficult to see every indentation clearly in the stone carving. Even his sunglasses were of little use. Cookie was not having any luck either so they changed places hoping one of them could spot something the other had missed.

Cookie strained to find something . . . anything. She was about to call it a day when she heard Hilton.

'Pssssssssst . . . Cookie, come here quick,' he called in a low voice.

Cookie ran over to join Hilton alongside the second lion.

'What?' she whispered, looking anxious.

'Look at this,' said Hilton pointing to the lion's mouth. 'Look inside . . . look at the tongue . . . way in the back.' Hilton looked around to ensure no one was watching. Cookie was trying desperately to see what he was talking about.

'Here . . . look,' said Hilton passing her the magnifying glass and pointing inside the lion's mouth, at something on the tongue.

'Yeah. What is it?' Cookie asked as she spotted an inscription, but it was too deep to get a good look at.

Hilton went into his backpack again and took out a piece of plain white writing paper, a pencil, and a small painter's brush. He gave the pencil and paper to Cookie to hold. He used the paint brush to whisk away dust and loose particles covering the marking. He then used all the wind he could muster and blew into the open mouth to clear the final bits of debris. The surface of the tongue was fairly smooth. He took the white writing paper and placed it over the marks on the surface of the tongue.

Holding down the paper, he made a pencil rubbing of the indented area. He started gently and slowly increased the pressure. Dark characters began to form on the paper.

Hilton removed the paper. Cookie smiled, impressed with Hilton's ingenuity. Three small symbols stood out on the paper, they were crystal clear.

The temple area was becoming more active and they decided to leave. Cookie followed Hilton as they rode back to the town centre.

A ferry was just docking as Hilton and Cookie made their way slowly through the crowded main street. Passengers were now departing the vessel and as the two teenagers cycled slowly past the congested area.

Fatty and Chopstick walked out of the shadow of the ferry terminal and onto the street.

'Do you think those little troublemakers are here yet?' Chopstick wondered.

'Well we know one thing for sure, they'll be here tomorrow,' replied Fatty. 'We'll keep an eye out for them around this area. They can't get off the boat without us spotting them and everyone comes by here sooner or later.'

'Yeah right. Like shooting fish in a barrel,' commented Chopstick. 'No escape for our little friends this time.'

Fatty and Chopstick crossed the street and sat down at an open-air café. They ordered some food, while carefully surveying the passers-by.

Hilton and Cookie headed towards Tung Wan Beach. Hilton had viewed the beach from the lookout pavilion and wanted to see it up close. Tomorrow was going to be exciting with the championship on the line. All the competitors would arrive tomorrow along with their equipment. Hilton was hoping to get in some last-minute practice early in the morning. They stopped at a small food stand, ordered some take out, and walked their bikes over to a shaded area with a table. They had a great view of the beachfront. They finished their lunch and disposed of their trash. Hilton sat back in his chair, looked around, and removed the rubbing from his pouch. Cookie moved closer so she could get a better look. Now they had to try and solve another puzzle.

'Look at this character,' said Hilton. 'This looks like *north*.'

Cookie took the paper from Hilton and sat back to

examine it more closely while Hilton was consumed in deep thought. Hilton broke from his concentration and pulled out the spyglass. He stood up and viewed the beach through the brass spyglass. He tried to relax and release his tension in the hope he could think more clearly.

'Hilton . . . I think these are numbers, maybe 44 and 38, and this could be east or west and this is definitely north,' said Cookie.

'Could be,' replied Hilton. 'But what does it all mean? This symbol here doesn't seem to go with any of the others.'

Cookie stood up to stretch, turning her shoulders to loosen her muscles. Suddenly she stopped. She was staring at Cheung Chau's famous banyan tree. This tree was said to be the dwelling place of the spirit of health. Cookie picked up the paper and walked over to the gnarled, old landmark.

Hilton had put in his earphones and turned on his MP3 player and closed his eyes. He sang along quietly to his favourite hip-hop songs. When he opened his eyes he saw that Cookie had vacated her seat. He sat up and looked around spotting her standing by the huge tree. He unplugged his earphones and went over to join her.

'What's up?' asked Hilton.

Cookie passed him the paper.

'Look, look at this symbol, the one that does not fit in with the others.'

Cookie took his arm and tugged him back to their table.

'Now look at the symbol and look at the tree,' said Cookie. 'Do you see it? This is not a Chinese character . . . this is a bad drawing of this tree.'

Hilton looked very closely at the tree and the symbol.

'Possible, very possible,' said Hilton. 'So, if we assume this symbol is this tree, where do all these numbers and directions fit in?'

Cookie shook her head, without an answer. Hilton began to pace back and forth. He looked at the tree, the beach-front, the roadway, and the coastline. Two hundred years ago none of these buildings would have been here. But the tree was at least two, most likely three hundred years old. Hilton had an idea.

'Let's try this,' said Hilton. 'Didn't the pirates always use paces as a form of measurement? A pace being a fairly large step of just under a metre. Since the pirates were seafaring men they used degrees to chart their courses. Cookie, you said the ghost was pointing or waving. Which hand did he use?'

Cookie thought for a while and tried to remember.

'His right hand,' replied Cookie. 'Yeah . . . for sure his right hand.'

Hilton thought aloud: 'He was facing you, using his right hand, that means he was pointing north. The Chinese character we took from the lion's mouth said north and the character on the silk flag mentioned north.

'So let's see. . . .'

Hilton stood level with the great spirit tree and began to count out 44 paces to the east. This led them towards the beach. He stopped on the spot and turned to the north, facing the opposite end of the island to Cheung Po Tsai's infamous cave. He tried to estimate an angle of 38 degrees. Using his arms to mark the desired angle, he found himself facing the coastline at the far end of the island. He really could not see anything distinct and stood there for awhile. He took out the spyglass, and began turning the front lens piece to adjust the focus. He turned it slowly and felt the lens piece click into place. Through the spyglass he could see an area about a kilometre away. Back towards the lookout pavilion, near the summit, on the hillside overlooking the rocky coastline of Sin Kung Tung. He watched it for a

few minutes and then handed the spyglass to Cookie. 'Do you see that area up on the hillside near the top?' asked Hilton. He tried to adjust the spyglass to the proper position.

'I think I see what you mean,' replied Cookie. 'Yeah . . . yeah . . . now I see it. Kind of a clearing with some large rocks surrounded by bushes and small trees.'

Hilton took back the spyglass and again focused on the area in question.

'I'm looking for some rocks or trees that we can use as markers so we can identify the area once we get up there,' said Hilton.

He studied the area through the spyglass and wrote every detail in his notebook. He made some crude drawings, shapes of trees and branches and closed the book.

'I think I can find that place now,' said Hilton blinking his eyes, as he put his sunglasses back on.

'Let's go,' said Cookie smiling, as she ran over to her bicycle.

Hilton placed everything in his backpack and got on his bike too.

'Cheung Po Tsai . . . get ready because here we come,' he whispered.

Chapter 10

FATTY AND CHOPSTICK HAD GROWN RESTLESS after watching people pass by for two hours, so they decided to go and check out the beach area. Tung Wan Road would lead them right to the site of Sunday's competition. As they approached the crowded beach, Chopstick noticed something out of the corner of his eye. He quickly ran back to the beachfront road and saw two riders who were now almost out of sight. He scratched his head. Fatty followed, running up to him and breathing heavily.

'What is it?' asked Fatty. 'Are you trying to kill me? Did you see something?'

'Those two kids on the bicycles kind of looked . . . I'm not sure.'

'Next time be sure,' snapped Fatty as he hit Chopstick with his hat. 'All that running could give me a heart attack. Keep your eyes peeled and pay attention. There are hundreds of kids here on bicycles. We can't go around chasing all of them.'

Hilton and Cookie rode back to the lookout pavilion. The road came to an abrupt end so they left their bikes and started their trek. They encountered thick brush and tangled trees making a fast advance almost impossible. The pushed their way through the foliage and after 20 minutes of fighting their way through the walls of wispy branches and tall grass they came to a very small clearing.

Hilton carried the notebook around with him as he

looked for the markers that would verify the exact location he had seen through the spyglass. After several minutes of searching and rechecking his notes he was satisfied they were in the right place.

'I'm pretty sure this is the place we saw through the spyglass,' proclaimed Hilton.

'Remember, digging is illegal, so I didn't bring any shovel. Easier to avoid the temptation.'

'Up here . . . who would know?'

'That's not the point,' replied Hilton. 'We have to respect the laws no matter who knows.' 'You're absolutely right Hilton,' agreed Cookie. 'Well . . . what are we looking for?'

'Look around carefully,' said Hilton. 'Try to imagine this area 200 years ago.

They both walked in circles, tugging at the small trees and trying to push over the large stones. They found nothing unusual and finally took a seat on a large flat rock. Frustration was setting in. There were supposed to be clues for them to find! So far the trip was a huge disappointment. How were they ever going to find the treasure? This was definitely 'mission impossible'.

Hilton took a bottle of cold lemon tea from his pack and offered it to Cookie. She had a long drink and handed it back to Hilton who took off his cap and poured the remainder of the bottle over his head.

'That hit the spot,' remarked Hilton calmly. 'Now I feel refreshed.'

'You're kind of stupid sometimes . . . you know that don't you?' said Cookie trying to hold back the laughter.

'Maybe we should get back to the bikes,' said

Hilton looking at his watch. 'We can go back to town centre, buy some food and a couple drinks, then come back here and try to figure this out.'

They got up and started to punch their way back through the tall grass and tangled branches. Hilton led the way, clearing a path for Cookie. He suddenly put on the brakes, raised his arm and blocked Cookie from proceeding. He turned to her and put his finger on his lips. He gently pushed down on her shoulder and slowly moved to the right, taking cover behind a large rock. Hilton pointed forward. Through the branches they could see two men, one fat, one skinny, looking very tired after their walk up the hill.

'I think those are the two guys who jumped us in Shatin,' whispered Hilton. 'One fat and one skinny, that's all I really remember. The sunglasses, the hats, all the same.'

'What are they doing here?' asked Cookie quietly. 'They can't possibly know who we are or why we are here. Why would they want to bother us?'

'I'm sure these are the same two guys who were hanging around our jeep the day we had to stop for that accident,' replied Hilton. 'I remember their colourful, flowered shirts . . . and they're wearing the same ones today.'

'Yeah . . . if you're going to try following someone the least you could do is change your shirt once in awhile,' quipped Cookie. 'I think that is probably the number one rule for creepy guys following kids.'

'Shhhh . . . just sit tight for a bit . . . see what they are up to.'

Fatty and Chopstick looked around the area,

appearing very harmless and acting casual. They walked over to the two bikes and Chopstick stood one up and got on the saddle. His long legs made it awkward for him to ride. He kept loosing his balance, got bored of riding in circles, so he got off leaving the bike near the other.

Hilton and Cookie gave each other a concerned look. The two mysterious men suddenly were heading in their direction. The twins moved behind the huge rock and slowly wiggled their way backwards through the underbrush, keeping an eye on the two men. Fatty stopped and Chopstick was not about to tackle the wall of branches. It appeared this was the end of the road for them.

Cookie continued to retreat until she stepped on a large, dry, tree branch, which broke with a resounding CRACK. The teens froze. Fatty and Chopstick looked at each other then peered in the direction of the sound. The men began to push slowly through the scrub and tall grass. Cookie and Hilton crouched as low as possible and moved quickly and silently back towards the clearing. They could hear the two men moving more quickly, making steady headway. Hilton reached the clearing first, grabbed Cookie's arm, and took her speedily across to the tall grass and brush on the opposite side. The grass was so high they could not see where they were going. Their hearts were racing, they had to get away. Hilton used his hands and arms to bat away the wall of grass, clearing the way. Cookie was right on his heels, matching him stride for stride.

Suddenly the thick brush ended and the earth beneath them gave way. They had come to the edge

of the cliff and could not stop their forward
momentum. They started to slide down the steep
bank but reacted quickly by grabbing some
overhanging branches. The twins had slid about three
metres below the edge of the cliff. They dangled
there, hearts beating a hundred miles an hour.

Far below the surf pounded the rocky coastline,
water spouting between the jagged rocks. Hilton
looked down at his feet and noticed a large stone
protruding from the cliff's face. He lowered himself
another half metre and was able to secure his balance
on the exposed rock. Cookie was terrified so Hilton
gently guided her to the secure, but uneven platform.
They held the branches for dear life and did not dare
to look down. Then voices could be heard from
above so they pressed themselves against the cliff
wall. Fatty and Chopstick were directly above them.
They waited for several minutes and soon the sound
of the voices could be heard fading away. They must
be leaving. The twins waited a while longer until
nothing could be heard from above.

'Don't move,' advised Hilton after a few minutes,
as he began to hoist himself up the branches and
back to the top of the cliff. Cookie was terrified.
Once there, he got out his rope from his backpack
and tied it around the trunk of a large tree. On the
other end of the rope he made a large loop and threw
it down to Cookie.

'Cookie, put this around your waist, close the
knot, hold onto those branches, and start climbing
back up,' instructed Hilton. 'I'll pull you up from
here. Don't be afraid, everything is going to be
alright. Let's go on the count of three: one . . . two . .

. three.'

Cookie began to climb and Hilton pulled. Cookie was quickly brought back to safety. They were both out of breath and speechless. Hilton took another bottle of lemon tea out of his backpack and was about to pour it over his head when Cookie quickly grabbed it from his hand and began drinking feverishly.

'Next time you decide to go running blindly through a forest remind me not to follow you,' she said angrily. 'Next time — if there is a next time — you follow me. You almost got us killed.'

'Killed . . . what do you mean? I saved our lives. Who knows what those guys are after,' replied Hilton. 'Great view though. I like it so much maybe I'll build a house up here one day.'

Hilton shook his head, exhausted from the terrifying ordeal. He tried to remain cool, but it wasn't easy.

They sat there for awhile to settle their nerves. Hilton got up, took a deep breath, adjusted his backpack, and was ready to leave. Cookie was still shaken and angry at Hilton. Hilton started in the direction of the bikes but Cookie decided to make her own pathway about ten metres to the right of Hilton. Hilton knew she was very upset so he just let her go her own way. She struggled with the tall grass and tangled branches. Hilton was moving more quickly as he took the path they had already carved through the wilderness. Hilton looked back and could see Cookie's outline through the vegetation. He could hear her stepping on dry twigs and they crackled beneath her feet. Hilton continued his way to the park and headed for the bicycles. He sat on a nearby bench and waited for Cookie.

Cookie moved slowly, becoming more frustrated with the thick growth. She unknowingly began to move further off course, not paying attention to her direction. Finally she fought her way through a wall of tall grass coming upon another tiny clearing. She had no idea where she was and was very tired. She had to rest.

Cookie paced about and beneath her feet she felt flat stones covered with brown, dry grass. The stones were not visible to the naked eye. She stepped carefully but stumbled many times as the stones were spaced unevenly. She stopped and thought this was quite amusing. With her feet she began to tap the grass, locating all the stones in the area. She danced on them like an arcade game, jumping from stone to stone. Cookie was trying to calm herself. Dancing on the hidden stones was kind of fun and her stress level was improving. She was getting caught up in the game when she suddenly stopped, sensing something was not right.

She froze in her tracks, suddenly afraid to move. Her instincts told her to run . . . get away immediately. She could not react quickly enough. There was a grinding sound, then nothing. The earth beneath her gave way and the black hole swallowed her up.

Chapter 11

HILTON WAITED IMPATIENTLY for Cookie. He knew she was upset with his careless action but usually did not act this childishly. After a few minutes, he sighed and started back towards the thick underbrush. Hilton played with his lucky shark tooth, hoping there were no more surprises in store. She just wanted him to come and get her. I'll play along, he thought. He moved the tall grass aside with his arms but still could not see Cookie. He could not hear anything. Silence. Where had she gone?

'All right I'm sorry . . . okay,' called Hilton. 'Stop playing games. Where are you?'

Hilton continued to thrash through the brush and branches but there was no sign of Cookie. He tried to retrace her steps. The grass had recently been flattened, so he was definitely on the right track. He pushed forward and into a clearing and stopped. Hilton saw the grass and bushes on the other side of the clearing had not been disturbed. If Cookie had reached this small clearing, then where was she?

Hilton walked around the area and felt stones under his feet. He was getting angry and frustrated thinking Cookie was playing a practical joke on him and did not appreciate it one bit. He thought this time she had gone too far with her foolishness.

'Okay Cookie . . . I'm phoning Uncle 6 to come here and help me look for you,' said Hilton loudly. 'Here I go . . . I'm punching in the numbers . . . you can come out now . . . I guess I'll just find the treasure by myself.'

Hilton took an awkward step, putting a lot of extra pressure on one of the stones, then let out a high-pitched yelp as he slid rapidly on his back, down a smooth, wet, mossy, stone chute. He could not see anything and was helpless to control his speed. There was nothing to grab on to. It was a roller-coaster ride under the most frightening conditions. His descent seemed to be getting faster and steeper. What was at the bottom? Jagged rocks . . . razor sharp spikes . . . a pit of poisonous snakes? He desperately tried to grab something, but the damp stone walls were too smooth. Suddenly he was airborne.

Hilton sailed through black space for a couple of seconds until his flight was abruptly halted, landing in a soggy, swamp-like bog with a loud, echoing splash. He was absolutely stunned. He grabbed his arms and legs to verify they were still in working order. What had just happened? Where was he? There was no telling how far down he had gone. Perhaps 20 metres or more. A few seconds passed, then a bright beam of light hit him directly in the face.

'It's about time you got here,' said Cookie. 'What took you so long?'

'Cookie, I was just going to phone you,' said an excited and relieved Hilton showing her his phone. 'Boy am I glad to see you.'

'I thought you were playing some kind of trick on me so I came back to look for you, retraced your steps. Guess I did a pretty good job, eh.'

'Very funny, genius. How are we going to get out of here?' asked Cookie.

Hilton got up from the bog and took out his large flashlight. He tried his mobile phone but there was no signal. Together they illuminated the darkness to discover they were inside a very large cavern. Hilton turned his light to the direction of the slippery chute. It was about three metres off the ground and there was no way to get back up there. The ceiling was very high and offered no sign of escape. He could see nothing he could tie his rope around in the hope of climbing back up the smooth stone chute. There was no sign of daylight anywhere. Their torches showed only one possible direction they could move. Taking positions on opposite sides of the eight-metre wide passageway, the twins started to walk slowly and carefully, as the footing was slippery and uneven.

'We must be a long way down,' said Hilton. 'I know I was moving forward. It felt like I was on that slide for about two minutes. I can't accurately judge the speed but I must have travelled three to four hundred metres. That would place us somewhere in the middle of the mountain.'

'Oh that's great news,' replied Cookie. 'How are we going to get out of this mess? First we almost go over a hundred-metre cliff, then we end up in the centre of the earth. I can't wait to see what happens next.'

Hilton took out his compass. He studied it for a second.

'Looks like we're going west . . . that's good,' said Hilton. 'West is heading back to the ocean, let's keep going.'

They forged ahead paying particular attention to their footing. Hilton counted their steps trying to gauge how far they might have gone. Cookie suddenly stopped and grabbed Hilton.

'Yikes Hilton, look!' shouted Cookie pointing with the beam of her flashlight.

The skeleton of a man hung on the cave wall. An arrow pierced the left eye socket of the skull. The sharp tip was solidly embedded in the stone wall. Hilton's light also showed several other arrows, broken and covered with slime, which had hit the wall and fallen to the ground around the skeleton. Hilton made his way over the Cookie's side of the cave.

'Be careful,' said Hilton as he stepped in front of Cookie. 'This passageway may be booby-trapped. Look at all those other arrows.'

Hilton inched his way towards the skeleton. He noticed a few other bones on the ground around the skeleton as it had fallen apart over the years, but none further along that side of the corridor. He remembered the stone plates that caused the earth to swallow them up only an hour ago. Hilton picked up some rocks and threw them on the cavern floor around the skeleton. Nothing happened.

'Let me try,' said Cookie picking up a larger stone. She used all her strength to heave it. The stone hit the floor near the skeleton with a resounding boom! There was an immediate grinding sound and then several arrows whistled from small holes located on the opposite side of the dark tunnel. They shattered upon hitting the stone wall, the cracking sound echoed throughout the cavern. Several arrows struck the skeleton causing it to explode all over the cave floor.

'Wow . . . I saw that in a movie once. We should be okay now,' said Hilton.

'After you,' said Cookie politely.

'Okay, okay, I'll go first,' said Hilton. 'Keep your light on the other wall just in case.'

Hilton moved cautiously towards the scattered bones, noting the positions where the deadly projectiles had been launched from. The hand from the shattered skeleton landed close to where they were standing. He crouched down to get a closer look.

'Gross,' said Cookie disgusted. 'I'm not touching that.'

Hilton noticed the fist of the man had not opened during impact. Very unusual considering the force which shattered the skeleton. He had obviously died clenching something. Hilton took out his boomerang and carefully tapped the hand trying to find the key to unlocking the finger joints. Finally, the bones fell apart revealing a small piece of paper. On closer examination, the paper displayed a symbol, very worn. It appeared to be a skull, a crimson skull. Hilton did not want to disturb the bones any further so he looked at the paper and copied the symbol in his notebook.

'What is it ?' asked Cookie.

'I don't know,' replied Hilton. 'Whatever it means . . . I guess it was worth getting himself killed for.'

They moved to the other side of the cave, ducking down below the firing line of the deadly arrows. They continued to move forward very cautiously.

The dark corridor started to narrow and the floor became dotted with an increasing number of muddy puddles.

'Maybe getting close to sea level . . . even worse, maybe below sea level. The floor of the cave seems to be getting really wet really fast. It's already covering our feet. I think we've been gradually going downward for quite a while,' said Hilton.

'What time is it?' asked Cookie with a serious tone in her voice.

'Why? Do you have another appointment perhaps, or missing your favourite soap opera?' quipped Hilton.

'What time is it?' she asked again firmly.

'It is 3:35 PM,' replied Hilton.

'Great . . . I noticed the high and low tides in the weather report this morning,' replied Cookie. She shone her flashlight on the cave wall, revealing a line about a metre above their heads.

'We have about one hour or so to get out of here. Look at the waterline,' said Cookie very seriously. 'In two or three hours this part of the cave will be completely under water.'

They quickened their pace and after about 20 minutes they seemed to run into a dead end. Hilton and Cookie could not believe their fate.

The water was already up to their knees and rising quickly. Hilton checked his watch and compass. He circled around flashing his light in all directions hoping to discover a way to continue forward. He had run out of ideas. Frustrated and tired, he leaned forward, put his hand on the muddy wall of the cave to hold himself up. His hand gave way on the slick surface and he lost his balance, falling to one knee, the water splashing him in the face. Cookie quickly turned towards Hilton to offer help. Cookie began tapping him repeatedly on the shoulder. He turned and she pointed at the granite wall behind him. His hand had wiped mud from the wall exposing the same symbol so tightly held in the grip of the skeleton's hand: the crimson skull!

Chapter 12

HILTON REGAINED HIS BALANCE and stood up. Using his shirt, he wiped the mud off his hand and quickly took out his notebook to show Cookie the drawing he had made earlier. Hilton knew they were a match and Cookie had a brief look to confirm their finding. They kept their lights focused on the wall. Hilton took a small towel from his backpack and began wiping a larger area around the marking. They took a few steps back to get a wider angle look at the symbol.

Cookie began to dance gingerly around, splashing water everywhere, hoping it might trigger, another secret opening. Hilton realised what she was doing and he began to press various areas of the stone wall surrounding the marking. He used the edge of his boomerang to search for a seam that would possibly show the outline of a hidden doorway. Nothing seemed to produce the desired results. In frustration Hilton picked up a football-sized stone and threw it hard at the wall, striking the symbol dead centre.

There was a loud grinding sound directly behind them. Slightly frightened, not knowing what was behind them, they turned around quickly. Their flashlights revealed part of the stone wall had revolved 90 degrees, creating a narrow opening about one metre off the ground. Was this another trap? Would there be more deadly arrows? The twins moved cautiously, shining their light through the open doorway and into the pitch-black hole.

'I'm not going in there,' stated Cookie loudly. 'Last time you almost got us killed, you go.'

'Okay, stay here,' replied Hilton. 'How long can you hold your breath?'

Cookie was upset but she knew Hilton was right. They had no other option but to go into the dark unknown once again. Hilton crawled up and headed in first, staying alert for any signs of danger. Cookie followed close behind. Finally they were through the opening and both stood upright. The grinding noise started again and they turned to see the stone door shutting. Hilton frantically looked for something to block the closing door.

He saw a wooden staff but it was too long. He leaned it against the wall and jumped on it. The staff broke in two and Hilton tried to wedge the piece between the base of the wall and the revolving stone door. The wood was no match for the huge piece of granite. The staff snapped like a toothpick.

Hilton ran to the door, slapping the stone slab in hope of locating a hidden release button. The stone door remained immobile. No way back to the outer cave now.

The teenagers' flashlights revealed an old torch stand near the wall. Hilton noticed a black, tarry substance covered with dust on the top of the torch pole. He took out a lighter and tried to ignite the black paste. It caught fire quickly, illuminating most of the room. They saw other torch brackets and followed the same procedure.

Before them was a stone stairway, littered with bones and broken crates. The twins ascended the thirteen steps to a large platform. They proceeded cautiously, alertly watching for any unwelcome surprises. The platform was well above the waterline, ensuring whatever was stored here would remain dry. The wall was scarred with hundreds of markings and curious drawings. Skulls and partial skeletons were scattered around the floor. Three rusted cannons were lined up against the wall and a vast assortment of dusty weapons covered in cobwebs were on display. Swords, knives, flintlock muskets, small pistols, and several blunderbuss rifles were scattered throughout. Brass telescopes, rope, and ammunition for the weapons were all organised in deteriorating wooden boxes. Cannon balls and kegs of gunpowder also made up part of the inventory. Hilton noticed a series of ropes dangling from the ceiling. He focused his light upwards to reveal what he thought were two wheels. He also notice the ceiling seemed to be moving.

Cookie shone her light upwards. 'What's that?'

No sooner had she spoken than they heard the sound of a thousand flapping wings. The sound level increased and huge cloud of small bats swooped down towards them. The twins ducked, knelt down, and curled into balls to avoid the surprise attack. The noise was ear-shattering and they could feel the wind from the bat's wings above their heads. This was scary. Thankfully, after a minute or so the bats returned to roost on the cave ceiling. Hilton and Cookie got to their feet and dusted themselves off.

'Why doesn't this surprise me?' said Cookie.

Hilton had more important things on his mind. 'I think those two wheels up there make up some kind of pulley system. Look at those ropes hanging over there,' he said.

'There's something else up there . . . can you see it?' asked Cookie.

'Looks like a big basket. Hold the light here so I can get these ropes untangled.'

'This must have been the pirates' storage room,' remarked Cookie. 'I bet all this stuff here is worth a lot of money.'

Hilton had the ropes organised in a straight line and he began to pull down on each one slowly to see how they would respond.

'This is their storeroom for sure,' agreed Hilton. 'And if that's the case there has got to be another way in and out of this cave. The bats have to go out to feed somehow. I sure hope these pirates were as smart as I think they were. They went to a lot of trouble to design and construct these tunnels and trap doors, they must have built another way in and out of here.'

Nothing Hilton did seemed to work. He was very careful, hoping not to break the old, dusty, ropes. Cookie came over and grabbed one of the ropes.

'When the vending machine at school won't work you hit it or kick it as hard as you can,' said Cookie. 'Like this.'

Cookie gave the rope a stern yank. They were showered with dirt and dust from above and out of the darkness a large basket was in free fall, heading right for them.

'Get out of the way!' yelled Hilton, pushing her

aside.

The basket came crashing to the floor just missing them. Cookie smiled and Hilton shook his head in disbelief.

'The elevator has arrived,' said Cookie.

Hilton and Cookie played with the ropes, locating the ones which would raise the basket. They both got in the basket and tried to pull.

The basket did not move.

'Cookie, you get out,' ordered Hilton.

'You get out,' replied Cookie quickly. But after a moment she reluctantly climbed out of the basket.

'You're not going to leave me down here. No way Hilton!' squeaked Cookie. 'I'm not as heavy as you, so I should get in the basket first — right?'

'Listen. I'm stronger, so when you pull on this rope I can also pull on the other rope while I'm in the basket. Together we should be able to get it off the ground. Hopefully there is an opening at the top somewhere. I can then pull you up. Don't be such a baby all the time.'

'All right then, let's go,' replied Cookie as she grabbed the rope. Hilton climbed inside and they both pulled together. The basket slowly started to rise.

'Cookie, pretend we're in the Dragon Boat races. We have to get into a rhythm so the ascent will be smooth. These ropes are very old and we don't want them to break or we'll never get out of here. Ready? Okay, together . . . pull . . . pull . . . pull.'

The basket rose steadily upwards. Hilton calculated about 30 metres to the top. About halfway up they were getting tired and slowed to a stop. Time for a little rest.

'Hold this position . . . rest for awhile so I can have a look around,' he shouted down to Cookie.

Hilton took his light and pointed it at the top of the cave to see if any opening could be detected. Nothing appeared obvious. He brought the beam of light downward along the wall. Something caught his attention. He backed up and stopped. The beam showed what looked like another red skull symbol about three metres above him.

'Cookie, a few more pulls. Stop . . . stop,' shouted Hilton.

It took almost a minute to cover the distance and now Hilton was face to face with the ominous marking. He examined the skull briefly. He thought he noticed a circle cut into the stone around the right eye of the skull but he was about a metre away and could not see clearly. Hilton thought best to continue the journey upwards and abandon the skull for now. They had to find a way out. He called Cookie to commence pulling on the rope. The basket moved closer to the top of the cave and finally came to a stop. Hilton saw a small stone landing area and got out of the basket. He put pressure on the protruding stone to ensure it was safe, then stepped completely out of the basket.

'What's going on up there?' shouted Cookie.

'Just a minute,' replied Hilton.

Hilton could see that the ceiling was completely enclosed. The bats had settled down so he could concentrate fully on his mission. Why would the basket stop here if there was no way out? He looked more carefully and saw a small, brick-shaped stone.

It looked out of place, not matching the other stones around it. A faded red skull was barely visible through a film of moist grime. Taking a chance, he pushed it. The stone wall began to part. He could now hear the ocean and feel the salt water breeze whistle through the narrow passageway.

'Cookie . . . Cookie . . . I think I've found the way out,' he shouted happily. 'I'll send down the basket.' Hilton lowered the basket to the bottom of the cave. Cookie steadied it on the granite floor and hastily climbed in. It took every ounce of energy they had left to pull the basket back to the top of the cave. The basket swayed slightly as Cookie arrived at the stone platform. Hilton grabbed her, helping her to firm footing.

'Can you feel that cool air . . . that is the sweet smell of freedom,' proudly announced Hilton.

'Let's get out of here.'

Hilton stopped on the other side of the doorway and noted another brick-like rock. Now he knew how to get back inside. Hilton led the way through the narrow corridor. They heard the granite door close behind them. The sound of crashing waves became much louder. Light streamed through the darkness up ahead. Finally they emerged through tight opening and they both took a deep breath of fresh air. They both let out a sigh of relief.

There was a grass-covered, crooked pathway leading down to a small inlet below. That must be where the pirates unloaded their supplies and chests of treasure. The entrance to the cave was covered with thick brush and totally invisible from the sea. You had to know exactly where it was or you could never find it. Hilton took a small white towel from his backpack and tied it at the base of small bush. This marker would make the cave entrance easier to identify upon their return. Hilton checked his compass and led Cookie up the hillside, eventually reaching the roadway. They arrived back at the lookout pavilion after a tiring walk and looked at each other and started laughing. The teens were a mess. Their clothes were wet, stained with mud and grass, their arms and legs were filthy. They pointed at each other's face where pieces of dirt and sod remained. Using their shirt sleeves, they wiped off some of the debris. Their bicycles were in the same place as they left them so the twins jumped aboard and rode back to town centre.

Uncle 6 was meeting them for dinner at a restaurant along the promenade. They arrived about 30 minutes early so they got a table with a great ocean view. The restaurant staff gave them some unusual looks so the brother and sister team headed for the washrooms to clean themselves up as best possible, but there wasn't much they could do about their clothes. They went back to their table and ordered a large cool drink each. Hilton related to Cookie what he had seen halfway up the wall. The twins had indeed discovered the pirate's secret storage room.

Cookie had been worrying about more historical relics, though. 'Those were the guys who attacked us at the KCR station,' she said. 'We have to tell the police!'

'Yes, but if we do it now our treasure hunt would be over. They'd fence off the whole area and maybe in a couple of years we'd read about some archaeologists discovering the "Treasure of Cheung Po Tsai". If we're smart we can handle those guys until we leave Cheung Chau. We have to give ourselves a chance to find it.'

The two teenagers continued their discussion quietly, completely unaware they were being watched from across the street. Fatty and Chopstick could not believe their good fortune.

'Can you believe this stroke of luck!' exclaimed Fatty adjusting his sunglasses.

'Keep an eye on them, we can't afford to lose them now,' continued Fatty. 'Big Brother is due tomorrow, we can't displease him again. . . .' Fatty pointed towards the twins as their uncle arrived.

Uncle 6 sat down, noting the twins' dirty clothes. 'You two look like you had quite a day, a lot of fun. Am I right?' asked Uncle 6 laughing. 'I knew you two wouldn't be bored and it looks like you weren't.'

Hilton and Cookie looked at each other.

'Oh yeah, we've had the time of our lives,' replied Cookie trying to smile.

'Most fun we've had in years. Can't wait to do it again tomorrow,' added Hilton.

Uncle 6 ordered dinner and they had a pleasant meal. The twins did not mention a word about their series of mishaps or their findings. Then dinner was over and the two adventurers were totally exhausted. They needed a good shower and a good night's sleep.

Hilton tried to focus on the windsurfing championship, but the thought of finding Cheung Po Tsai's treasure kept invading his mind with visions of untold wealth and fame. The teens knew tomorrow was going to be a very interesting day. Very interesting indeed!

Chapter 13

HILTON AND COOKIE GOT BACK TO THEIR ROOMS, had a much-needed shower and sat down to quietly discuss the day's events. They were obsessed with finding the treasure now. The twins had a feeling they were getting close and nothing was going to stop them, nothing. Everything pointed to the secret of the treasure being somewhere in the pirate's storage cave. The small cove for docking a boat, a narrow pathway up the hillside, a cave entrance completely hidden from view, and an elaborate pulley system for transporting goods and people in and out of the cave.

The twins also discussed the two men they had seen at the pavilion. Their appearance on the island was no accident. Maybe they knew something about the pirate's treasure as well? They could not take any chances and devised a plan just in case their suspicions were correct.

The family and their friends would be on the island tomorrow to cheer on Hilton during the windsurfing championship. Hilton told Cookie he would be leaving for the beach early to prepare his equipment and get in some practice. He had to get used to the wave patterns and wind direction in order to decide his strategy.

Next morning Hilton was up early, organising his backpack, only taking items he needed for the competition. In the kitchen he helped himself to a bowl of congee and went out the door where he greeted Uncle 6 who was in the garden attending to his orchids. Uncle 6 wished him good luck and Hilton was on his way. It was only a fifteen-minute walk to the beach and Hilton needed the exercise to loosen his muscles.

A hundred metres behind Hilton two men stood in a doorway alcove, half-asleep on their feet. Fatty had one eye on the roadway. He quickly jerked forward and slapped Chopstick.

'What . . . what?' asked Chopstick, rubbing his tired eyes.

'Look. The kid, he's leaving,' said Fatty.

'Let's follow him,' said Chopstick. 'There's no one around, we can get him easy.'

'Just a minute,' replied Fatty. 'Where's the girl? They're always together. We know where he's going, he's in that stupid windsurfing thing. Let's wait, we'll get the girl, use her for bait. Then he'll have no choice but to bring us the spyglass.'

'Great idea Fatty,' replied Chopstick. 'Now I can get some more sleep.'

Fatty looked over at Chopstick with disgust.

At the beach, Hilton looked around casually to see if Rico Wong had arrived, but he could not locate him. He gathered his equipment and started checking it out. It would be just like Rico to make a late entrance, purposely drawing all the attention in his direction. Mister Big Shot was much too cocky and there was no way Hilton was going to lose this championship to him. If Rico won today, Hilton would never hear the end of it. Listening to Rico brag for a whole season would be too much for anyone to stomach. Hilton knew he had to focus on the task at hand, so sunglasses on, try to relax, get in the zone. The proper mindset was the key. Hilton knew he had the ability. He kept telling himself this was going to be his day. MP3 player and hip-hop music. Earphones in. Volume up. Perfect.

About an hour and a half later, Cookie emerged from the flat and walked out to the roadway. Chopstick was the watchdog this time and came to life. He nudged Fatty who awoke quickly. Cookie stopped at the roadside and pretended to adjust her backpack, while she looked up and down the street to see if there was anyone or anything out of the ordinary. She stopped, took out her makeup bag and used her small mirror to see what was going on behind her. She observed two suspicious men shuffling around in a doorway. She casually walked down the roadway onto the main street and rented a bicycle. Fatty and Chopstick followed, but Cookie got on the bike and quickly pedalled off.

'She's getting away,' cried Chopstick.

Both men ran towards the bicycle stall. They rented two bicycles and awkwardly began to follow Cookie. She took a quick look behind and saw the two men struggling with their poor riding techniques. They bumped into each other many times, losing their balance and coming to a halt, yelling at each other, only to angrily start their pursuit once again. Cookie smiled and continued her ride along Cheung Chau's pretty harbour side promenade. She rounded the bend and looking over her shoulder saw Fatty hit the curb and almost go into the water. Chopstick grabbed him in the nick of time and pulled him upright.

Cookie continued to lead them on a merry chase. She left her bike at the bottom of the hill leading up to the cave of Cheung Po Tsai, and headed up on foot.

The two men saw her dismount and hurried to make up the distance between them. Cookie kept a watchful eye on the two bikes and deliberately slowed her pace so they could catch up. She started up the cement pathway leading to the cave. She was now out of their sight heading towards the cave. Cookie heard them drop their bikes on the cement roadway at the bottom of the hill. The two men, weak kneed, began the trek up the pathway. She stayed about 30 metres ahead of them so they could just barely see her as she made her way to the summit.

Behind her the two men stepped quietly trying not to be too obvious. Cookie passed an outdoor restroom, continued and finally reached the end of the pathway and turned the corner out of sight.

The two very out-of-shape men were exhausted by the time they reached the public toilet.

'I got to go,' said Chopstick.

'Not now, you idiot,' replied Fatty in a harsh whisper. 'She's just up there, all alone. This our big chance to get her and find out where that spyglass is. Get going you dummy.'

Cookie stepped into the entrance of the cave and waited. A few moments later she heard the shuffling of feet and knew the two men were about to turn the corner. They stopped and peeked around the corner of the large boulder only to see Cookie disappear inside the pirate's cave.

'Come on,' whispered Fatty. 'We've got her trapped, get in there.'

Fatty pushed Chopstick forward towards the dark opening. Chopstick hesitated, looking very unsure of the situation. Fatty continued to force him towards the black hole. Chopstick was a very reluctant volunteer, but entered gingerly. Fatty stayed close behind so there was no way for him to retreat.

'Okay, okay,' said Chopstick nervously. 'You know I sleep with my night light on, it looks kind of dark in there. I don't like this.'

'Shut up and get moving. I'm right behind you. Hurry up!' ordered Fatty.

They made their way cautiously down the steel ladder and into the darkness.

Cookie could hear them moving about behind her. She made some subtle noises to let them know she was up ahead. They gangsters had no flashlights. It was the blind leading the blind. Fatty could barely fit through the opening to the cave. The men could only feel their way along the damp stone corridor and had no idea the chamber was about to become very narrow. Cookie climbed up the second small, steel ladder which would lead her to the exit of the cave. She made some more noise hoping they would continue their pursuit. Chopstick guided Fatty through the blackness, but it was getting narrower and more awkward even for him.

'I can't get through, I think she's just up ahead, I heard her,' said Fatty. 'Help me you idiot, pull me forward.'

Chopstick was in very cramped quarters but managed to turn halfway around and started to pull Fatty in an effort to squeeze him further through the passageway.

'I'm stuck you moron, stop pulling, you're ripping my arms out,' said Fatty madly.

'I can't go any further either,' proclaimed Chopstick. 'I'm too tall and I can't see where I'm going.'

'Where's that little brat, she's got to be in here somewhere,' said Fatty struggling to get the words out. 'How could she vanish like that? I can't move.'

'Go back, go back,' said Chopstick. 'Let's get out of here and wait for her to come out.'

'I can't move, I'm jammed in here,' replied Fatty.

'I'll push you out,' Chopstick suggested.

Chopstick tried his best to force Fatty backwards. There was no movement, only Fatty's cries of pain. He was wedged between the narrow walls totally blocking the way back to the entrance of the cave. Chopstick could not move forward because of his height and long legs. They were in total darkness. Cookie was at the cave exit listening closely to their predicament. She and Hilton had planned this little escapade last night just in case. They hadn't been sure it would be effective, but it had worked to perfection. Their two unknown assailants were caged up like battery hens. Cookie's job was done.

'Well guys I'm off now,' she whispered sarcastically. 'Have a nice day.'

She made her way back to the main path and started down the hill to retrieve her bike and rode off to the windsurfing competition.

'Fatty are we ever going to get out of here?' asked Chopstick. 'Uh . . . remember I told you I had to use the toilet?'

'Shut up. You're driving me crazy,' replied Fatty. 'Whose dumb idea was it to follow that rotten kid in here.'

'Yours Fatty,' said Chopstick. 'I think it was yours, yeah, definitely yours.'

'If I ever get out of here I'm . . . .' yelled Fatty. He was abruptly interrupted by his mobile phone ringing.

Fatty tried to get his hand into his pocket but he was squeezed too tightly.

'Chopstick, get the phone out of my pocket,' ordered Fatty.

Chopstick reached into Fatty's pocket.

'Not that pocket you dummy,' shouted Fatty. 'Hey . . . hey . . . watch it numb skull, watch your hands.'

'Whoops, sorry about that,' replied Chopstick as he continued to search for the ringing phone.

'Got it,' announced Chopstick as he pressed the button and put it up to Fatty's ear.

Fatty started to tremble. 'Yes . . . yes . . . oh . . . everything's fine,' he said, trying to be calm. 'In fact we've located those kids and they are going to be at some kind of competition this afternoon. You know boss, these little monsters are mean and cruel but don't worry, you know us, we're a lot smarter than them . . . right boss . . . right.

'Big Brother, by any chance do you know how to get to this Cheung Po Tsai Cave?' asked Fatty. 'We thought we'd have a look and . . . well . . . it is really dark and narrow in here... and....'

116

Fatty went silent. Chopstick put the phone to his ear and there was nothing.

'What did he say?' asked Chopstick. 'He just got off the ferry and he'll be here after lunch, an hour or two. But he said have a nice time. He didn't sound like he really meant it. I think he's going to kill us,' replied Fatty.

'Speaking of lunch, I'm kind of getting hungry, how about you Fatty?'

Fatty growled and finally Chopstick was silent. All they could do is wait in the cool, damp, darkness.

They knew Big Brother was not going to be happy when he saw them.

Chapter 14

HILTON WAS ON THE BEACH checking his sailboard, to make sure it was in perfect working order for the big event. All the other competitors were doing likewise. Hilton liked to be away from the other contestants on race day so he could focus on what he had to do. Hip-hop music helped him block out everything else. He liked to visualise the entire run in his mind so nothing would surprise him when his chance came. Hilton glanced over at the large scoreboard as the judges were drawing for starting positions. He saw his name being placed on position number nine. Rico Wong got position ten. They would be the final two competitors of the day and the only two with a chance to win the championship. Hilton continued his preparation then suddenly noticed a dark shadow cover his board. He stared back into the bright sun to see someone directly behind him.

'Rico, finally made it, what's up man?' asked Hilton, returning to his work.

'Well buddy-boy, I see you're hard at it as usual,' replied Rico. 'Make sure you wax every inch. You're going to need all the help you can get.'

Hilton tried to ignore him but Rico was not about to leave.

'Don't you have something to do, someplace to go, far, very far, away. Maybe practise a little?' asked Hilton.

'We're the last two competitors, no rush, I have

lots of time,' replied Rico smugly. 'Practice . . . how much practice do you need to beat this bunch of nobodies. I only have to concentrate on one guy . . . don't I?'

Hilton smiled at the backhanded compliment, not acknowledging Rico at all.

'Okay, alright . . . if you were someone else it would have been nice talking to you, but you're not, so see you at the award ceremony,' said Hilton as he stood up to leave for the water. 'You go take a nap, talk to your friends, go fishing, do whatever you want, oh, and good luck today.'

'Luck, who needs luck?' replied Rico quickly as Hilton began to drag his board to the shoreline.

'You're the one who needs the luck . . . shark boy,' quipped Rico loudly. 'See you in the winner's circle, you'll be standing next to me, shaking my hand. I might even let you touch my trophy, but only if you ask nice.'

Hilton waved goodbye in a half-hearted motion and made his way into the water. He practised for about 30 minutes and then all the other windsurfers got into the water so he decided it was time for him to get out and just watch everyone else. He waited for Rico to catch his first good wave and studied his every move. Hilton knew he had to perform to the best of his ability today. As much as he hated to admit it, Rico was very good and if things went his way, could easily win. That little conversation on the beach showed Hilton that Rico was only concerned about him, no one else. Rico was the one who was worried. Hilton knew if he could post a really good score, Rico would have a lot of pressure on his shoulders, being the final competitor with one chance to win the championship. Let's see how Rico handles the challenge. May the best man win.

Everyone was arriving now. His parents, Uncle 6 and Markus spotted Hilton and walked up to greet him.

'Are you all ready, son?' asked Julien proudly.

'Of course dad,' replied Hilton. 'Hi mom, hi Uncle 6, hi Marcus. Wish me luck big guy, give me five.'

Marcus saluted his hero and grinned from ear to ear.

'Can I touch your shark tooth Hilton?' asked Markus.

'Sure can. Rub it for good luck,' instructed Hilton.

'Let's get a seat,' said Robyn. 'Where's your sister?'

'Right here mom,' called Cookie, jogging up from behind. 'Just doing a little sightseeing.'

The group wished Hilton good luck and headed for the bleachers. Cookie stayed on the beach with Hilton.

'Any problems?' asked Hilton.

'Not really,' replied Cookie smiling. 'Everything went according to plan. The two rocket scientists took the bait and now they're busy exploring Cheung Po Tsai's damp, dark, very, very narrow, cave. I don't think we'll see them for awhile.'

'Good girl,' said Hilton. The competition was about to start. The contestants were called out in order and tried their best to improve their place in the overall standings. There was still a prize for third place so everyone wanted to put in a good performance. T-Rex and Zack ran up to greet Hilton. Echo and Sammie tagged along with Carson and Ashley. The twins visited with their friends on the beach but Hilton was keeping a close eye on the size of the waves and wind direction. Zack and T-Rex knew the importance of this day so they let Hilton have some space to gather his thoughts. They all agreed to get together later that evening for an island barbecue. Hopefully a victory barbecue.

The afternoon moved along quickly and the public address system called the eighth competitor to get ready for his run. Hilton glanced over at Rico surrounded by his group of supporters and Rico was staring directly at Hilton. Rico had his usual cocky, confident smile on display for all to see. He tipped his sunglasses to acknowledge Hilton's glance, trying to look cool as a cucumber. Hilton believed underneath that calm was nothing but mounting fear. The PA announced: Competitor number nine — Hilton Chan. His family stood up and applauded. All his friends cheered loudly as Hilton went into the water and was towed out to the course. T-Rex had brought an air horn and let out a loud blast. Everyone covered their ears.

Zack, T-Rex, Echo, and Sammie, were joined by Carson and Ashley, ready to view the action. They all took out their binoculars to get a closer look.

Hilton was now out on the course, waiting for the start signal. There it was! Time to show everyone who's the best, who's the man. He stood up on the board and quickly established his balance. He manoeuvred his sail to take advantage of the favourable wind and started his run. He was moving very smoothly. The water beneath him seemed to form a perfect channel and he rode it flawlessly. He got a couple of nice waves and pulled off his trademark jumps to perfection. Hilton was in total control, he was in the zone. He zigzagged across the water like a ballroom dancer doing a brisk tango, waiting patiently for a big wave so he could attempt a flying loop. This would be a bold move but he needed the right conditions. There was not much time left. He looked over his shoulder and saw a large wave coming up behind him. This was it.

Those final few seconds seemed like hours. Suddenly he felt a nudge against his board. He nervously looked down, recalling the monster that stalked him at Stanley Beach. He did not see anything but quickly looked around for a dorsal fin. Hilton knew Tung Wan Beach was equipped with shark nets, but there was still reason for concern. It couldn't be another shark, impossible he thought. He kept telling himself to focus and concentrate. He rubbed his shark tooth for good luck. He felt the big wave coming and quickly abandoned all thoughts of the so-called ghost shark.

He rode the wave, shifted his weight quickly and started his attempt at a 360-degree loop. He landed roughly but recovered nicely. Everyone one the beach went crazy, shouting wildly in support of the outstanding stunt. Even Rico and his friends were amazed. They all looked at each other and started slapping Rico on the back for encouragement. Rico did not move, he kept up his cool outward appearance. Hilton headed for shore, ending his run in spectacular fashion. His friends ran to meet him at the shoreline, crowding around him in celebration. Rico did not look over at them. He waited for his number to be called and made his way out to the course.

Hilton had to smile. He knew even Rico's very best might not be good enough. Rico sat in the water and waited until Hilton's score was posted. He knew what he had to beat and was ready to go. Rico had to pull out all the stops. This was going to be no easy win today. Rico started his run, making jumps and quick turns on every wave no matter how large. He was putting on quite a show and Hilton could not detect any sign of hesitation. Hilton hated to admit it, but deep inside he knew there was not much between them when it came to windsurfing skill.

Rico continued his eye-catching routine and his confidence was building with every move. He was about to perform his signature trick when he felt a bump to his board from beneath, then another. He thought he had hit a piece of floating wood or debris. The sudden jolt disturbed his timing but he recovered quickly and adjusted. Then it happened again. He felt his sailboard lift slightly out of the water. Then another bump to the side of his board caused him to wobble, barely maintaining his balance. He angrily looked down into the water to witness a huge, dark shadow directly beneath him. He was shocked and swerved to get out of its way. Rico glanced to the rear. A gigantic fin was breaking the surface like a nuclear submarine surfacing from below. The shadow of death was there and on the move, zeroing in on Rico. The monster was gaining quickly and Rico knew he could not outrun this monster. Rico's heart was racing and a rush of adrenaline blocked out his thoughts. For a split second he only saw blackness. His hand came loose from the sail and he felt weightless, and dizzy.

On shore Hilton and his group could see something was wrong.

Rico had seemingly aborted his routine and was now moving about in a very uncharacteristic manner. Hilton saw him lose his grip on the sail, one hand waving about wildly, and one foot dangling in the water. He looked terribly off balance. He looked ready to fall.

Back at the cave, Fatty and Chopstick were falling asleep in the silent darkness when they heard the sound of someone near the entrance. The two men braced themselves, for they knew Big Brother was here. A bright light hit Fatty directly in the face. He turned sideways. There stood Big Brother. The criminal boss was short and stocky, neatly dressed in a white summer suit, tailor-made shirt open at the collar, sporting a stylish, matching white hat. His face was a different matter, displaying impatience and an ever-present scowl. He was seemingly always in a bad mood, especially around Fatty and Chopstick. He balanced himself inside the cave with his favourite walking stick. He stood there quietly for a moment, then broke the silence by cracking the walking stick against the stone wall. The echo startled the two captives and Big Brother shook his head in disgust.

'Well, well, could I possibly expect anything less?' came Big Brother's raspy, sarcastic voice. 'You two must be the biggest dummies in Hong Kong letting a couple school kids trap you like this.'

'We were just checking out the cave boss, it's a tourist attraction, you know,' replied Fatty.

'Who do you think you're talking to?' shouted Big Brother angrily. 'You're the only two clowns to ever get stuck in a tourist attraction. When are you ever going to smarten up?'

'Good to see you boss,' said Chopstick from the other side of Fatty.

'Shut up you idiot,' replied Big Brother firmly. 'Let's get you out of here, we have work to do.'

'You're not going to take us fishing are you boss?' asked Chopstick, trembling.

Big Brother grabbed Fatty and with a vicious yank, pulled him clear from the narrow passage.

'I'll take you fishing all right. The sharks wouldn't even bother to eat two boneheads like you, the sharks would get indigestion,' answered Big Brother. 'You are both equally useless. Matching bookends — stupid and stupider.'

Big Brother was very angry as he led the two incompetent gangsters out of the cave. They both winced once in the bright sunlight, taking a few minutes for their eyes to adjust. Fatty examined the many small scratches on his chubby arms and rolled up his lip like a little kid.

'We know exactly where the kids are Big Brother, I'll lead the way,' offered Fatty.

The three men slowly made their way down the pathway back to where they had left their bicycles.

Out in the ocean, Rico was regaining his senses. He grabbed onto the sail with both hands. Rico could see the shark as it moved back and forth underneath the board. The deadly monster seemed to be purposely terrorising him, there was no way to tell when the creature would deliver the death blow. Without notice the savage killer disappeared. Rico feared it had gone down deeper in order to launch a charge to the surface. Rico waited, his entire body covered with goose bumps. He felt ice cold. He had never experienced such fear and felt totally helpless.

Suddenly, the massive form could be seen rising from the deeper water, coming upwards faster and faster. Rico timed his move perfectly and used all his skill to avoid a fatal collision. The shark crashed through the surf with jagged jaws agape. A life-saving gust of wind took Rico 90 degrees right. The great killer gave Rico the 'death stare' as it sank below the surface and circled in the opposite direction. The winds were in Rico's favour and he made a run for it. Getting closer to the shoreline he turned to witness the great beast following him into the shallow water.

As Rico cruised into water less than a metre deep the giant shark turned smoothly and disappeared into the safety of deeper waters. Rico jumped from his board and frantically splashed his way to shore. He collapsed on the sand knowing he was finally out of danger.

Rico's friends rushed over to find out what happened. He was unable to speak and lay face down in the sand, saying nothing. A few moments later, Rico rolled over looking pale and sickly. He struggled to sit up and glanced over at the judges who were about to post his score. It was surprisingly good, but not good enough. He knew the outcome immediately. His head sank down.

When Hilton saw the final score he jumped, pumping his fist in the air as a victory salute. His family rushed down from their seats to congratulate him and his friends were all cheers and hugs. Cookie was dancing around in the sand. Rico looked up and nodded. He was devastated and still in shock. Could this shark have been the same one Hilton encountered at Stanley? He did not like many things about Hilton but he learned one thing for sure, he was no liar.

The announcer asked the competitors to come up to the podium for the presentation. Rico slowly made his way to where the top three point getters for the season received their gold, silver, and bronze medals. All the contestants received a small trophy and many pictures were taken. Rico moved slowly, still white as a ghost. Hilton shifted his attitude into 'cool' overdrive as he shook hands with the other winners as they stepped onto the platform. He felt a huge rush of energy and at the same time quietly let out a great sigh of relief. He had no idea what happened to Rico out there and was not about to ask. It was his time to bask in the glory of sweet victory. This was a just reward for what happened at Stanley Beach. The club president offered congratulations to all the competitors for a wonderful season. The competitors shook hands once more and the crowds began to disperse.

'What a fantastic day, couldn't get any better,'

exclaimed Cookie, winking at Hilton.

'Fantastic . . . thanks to everyone for your support, it really helped, thanks guys,' said Hilton in a very humble manner. Hilton rubbed his lucky shark tooth and looked skyward.

Hilton's eye caught the attention of Rachel, Cookie's schoolmate, standing at the back of the pack.

'Well hotshot, I might have mentioned something to Rachel about a big barbecue,' said Cookie. 'You can thank me later.'

'Anybody up for the greatest barbecue Cheung Chau has ever seen?' shouted a joyful T-Rex.

There was a loud, unified yes. The family congratulated Hilton again and he got a big hug from mom. He was a little embarrassed but took it in stride.

'That was very impressive son,' remarked Julien. 'We're going to take Uncle 6 to dinner tonight so you two enjoy the barbecue with your friends.'

'Thanks dad, we'll go back to the flat to get cleaned up and then join everyone back at the beach in about two hours,' said Hilton.

Further up the beach, three men had just arrived. Chopstick got out his binoculars and began scanning the beach.

'There they are, I got them, right over there,' said Chopstick pointing.

Big Brother grabbed his extended arm and threw it down to his side.

'Don't be so obvious, keep an eye on them,' said Big Brother. 'Don't let them out of your sight.'

Everyone headed back towards the town centre. Hilton and Cookie waved goodbye to their friends as they separated from the group. The family went back to Uncle 6's flat where they could freshen up. Hilton and Cookie's friends invaded the grocery stores and convenience shops looking for beverages, meats, buns, corn on the cob, and anything else they thought would make the world's best barbecue.

Hilton showered quickly, and loaded up his backpack. The twins stepped into the living room to say goodbye and Hilton quietly handed his father a small note. They were off. The two treasure hunters only had a couple hours to see if their theory about the secret entrance to the pirate's cave was correct. They rented bikes and headed up the promenade towards the lookout pavilion and the entrance to Cheung Po Tsai's most secret chamber.

Chapter 15

HILTON AND COOKIE PEDALLED up the hill, finally arriving at the pavilion. They leaned their bicycles against a large tree then surveyed the area, ensuring there were no followers. Once sure the coast was clear they made their way to the hillside and started down the grassy, narrow pathway. It required careful navigation as a slip would take them down the slope and over the cliff to the rocks below. Hilton knew they were getting close and kept eyes open for the towel he had affixed to the bush. Finally he spotted it fluttering in the sea breeze up ahead. He pointed it out to Cookie and they hurried to the location.

The twins pushed away the bushes that concealed the entrance. They stepped inside, and walked down the dark corridor until they came to a wall. Hilton found the pressure plate, the brick-like stone with the small crimson skull. He pushed it and the rock wall opened, exposing the small stone platform. The basket was right where they had left it.

'Cookie, you stay here and make sure the pulley system doesn't get jammed,' instructed Hilton. 'I'll lower myself down and when I reach spot on the cave wall I'll need you to hold the rope and steady the basket. I need to give that area a thorough examination. I believe we are getting close, real close. Wish me luck.'

'Okay, get going, see what you can find,' replied Cookie anxiously.

Hilton got into the basket and slowly descended into the forbidding darkness. Cookie could only see the beam from his flashlight below. She attended to the ropes, keeping them straight and making sure they would not tangle. Hilton scanned the damp, stone wall for the unusual marking he had noticed previously.

Then he saw it. Only a few more metres to go.

'Cookie, grab the rope . . . okay stop, I'm here,' shouted Hilton.

Cookie took hold of the ropes and brought the basket to a halt. She could faintly see Hilton's beam of light in the distance below. He was a long way down. Hilton focused on the cryptic symbol. Was this really the key the Cheung Po Tsai's hidden treasure?

Back at town centre, Chopstick had been relegated to rickshaw driver as Big Brother sat comfortably in the passenger seat. Fatty had been assigned to walk alongside. They had been following the twins from a safe distance, but now they were no longer in sight.

'The only thing up there is a lookout pavilion,' said Fatty. 'It's kind of a dead end so they should be easy to find.'

Chopstick strained to pick up the pace and Fatty had to jog to keep up with the bicycle rickshaw. They reached the pavilion, stopped, and Big Brother got down from his seat. Fatty collapsed on the ground and Chopstick was bent over gasping. Big Brother looked at both of them and shook his head.

'If you two weren't my nephews, I would disown you,' said Big Brother firmly. 'You are absolutely hopeless. Where are those kids? They're gone already.'

Fatty struggled to his feet and looked in all directions. Chopstick straightened up and tried to focus his blurry eyes. Fatty pointed to the other side of the clearing.

'Their bicycles are right there, they can't be too far away,' he said.

'We'll find them boss, don't worry,' added Fatty.

Inside the cave, Hilton took out the printout of the flag. The symbol on the wall looked very much like the eyes of the person pictured on the front of the flag. Was the image on the flag that of Cheung Po Tsai? The eyes on the front of the cloth matched up exactly with the skull symbols on the map side of the fabric. Hilton recalled what Cookie had told him after seeing the apparition. The ghost apparently had a black patch over its right eye. The pirate's right eye was hidden, just as the treasure had been hidden for over 200 years. Was that a clue to the puzzle?

Hilton brought out the spyglass that had led them on this adventure in the first place. He removed the flag and unfolded it. Hilton stretched it out, lining up the face on the flag with skull on the wall. The eyes lined up perfectly. The eyes must be the key. Hilton was certain of that. He took off the front eyepiece of the spyglass to use as a magnifying glass and studied the eerie symbol. Around what looked like the pupil of the right eye, there seemed to be a very fine, circular incision. He became excited at the discovery and tried to press it, hoping the pressure would release a secret entrance. Nothing happened and his excitement simmered. He knew he was very, very close to solving the mystery. What was the last piece of the puzzle?

'What are you doing down there?' asked Cookie impatiently. 'Are you okay, do you need anything?'

'I'm fine, just checking something,' replied Hilton. 'You okay up there?'

He could see her outline standing on the stone platform above. She looked fine. He was almost ready to give up, when out of nowhere, like a bolt of lightning, it came to him.

Hilton held the eyepiece up to the light so he could study it closely. The inner edge appeared to be quite sharp. He turned to the wall and placed the eyepiece over the right eye hole of the skull. He pressed gently and to his surprise the eyepiece slid into the circular seam very easily.

His imagination began to run wild once again, his heart beating faster. The eyepiece was literally a key. A key that would unlock the secret to lost treasure of Cheung Po Tsai.

'Open Sesame,' said Hilton quietly to himself.

He gave the eyepiece a gentle turn and heard a distinct click! The now-familiar sound of grinding stones were music to his ears. The wall opened, revealing another entrance into uncharted darkness.

'Cookie, I've found something,' shouted Hilton.

Without waiting for a response from above, he pulled on the ropes, raising the basket slightly. Now he was level with the entrance. He pulled himself over and crawled out of the basket, onto the granite floor. He remembered the corridor of arrows somewhere far below and the skeleton of the young man. Motionless, he used his flashlight to survey the area. He spotted a torch pole a few steps ahead, got to his feet, took it and lit it. The landing was bare but off to one side was another dark, narrow, hallway.

Hilton moved forward cautiously, fearful the entrance could be booby-trapped. He hesitated, uncertain of how he should proceed.

Hilton took one step further. Without notice the floor beneath him opened. He fell, his feet dangling in space but he reacted quickly, grabbing the edge of the opening. Below he could hear noises. Something was definitely moving down there. He lifted himself back to the safety of solid ground and used his flashlight to illuminate the dark pit.

The floor of the pit was covered with scorpions, thousands of scorpions. There were three skulls and a scattering of bones between the iron spikes that protruded from the floor. The would-be thieves had met a horrifying death. Hilton's heart was pounding. He moved away from the trap door quickly and it closed. He had come this far, there was no turning back now. He knew he was close to something, he could sense it. Who would go to all this trouble to protect nothing of value? He took a deep breath and continued forward. The pitch-black corridor was only a few paces long and opened into a larger area. Hilton found two other torch poles and brought them to life.

He turned around and came face to face with Cheung Po Tsai.

A huge flag, identical to the one in Hilton's spyglass was mounted on the wall of the cave. The time-worn image of Cheung Po Tsai looked down on three stone podiums. A large wooden chest was on the centre podium, flanked by two smaller ones.

The three chests with tarnished inlaid metal support straps had leather handles on either side, and were covered with dust and cobwebs. Large metal padlocks secured the contents.

Hilton looked around the chamber. The walls were adorned with whalebone daggers and crossed swords. Pistols and muskets were mounted on iron pegs. Maps depicting naval battles were displayed on the walls. Hilton moved closer to examine his findings and inspect the chests. He reached into his backpack and found his small tool kit.

With a jewellers screwdriver, he tried to pick the lock using a delicate approach. No luck, it remained firm. He again inserted the small tool and with a firm jerk, broke the locking mechanism. He removed the lock from the metal clasp and set it on the stone altar. He repeated the procedure with the other two chests and now they were all ready for his inspection. The contents were about to be exposed possibly for the first time in 200 years.

Hilton's heart began to pound rapidly. He stepped in front of the largest chest. The moment of truth was upon him. Was this really the treasure he had seen in his dreams or would these chests be filled only with musty air and lost hope, empty, bone-dry?

The rusty metal hinges squeaked as Hilton opened the first chest. He staggered backwards in awe. Before his eyes was indeed a king's ransom. Rings, bracelets, necklaces, and chops, made from the finest quality jade. Pearls, emeralds, and brilliant ornaments made of solid gold. Hilton's mouth was dry and he could not generate one single word or shout of joy. He was overwhelmed, speechless. He could not feel or hear anything. For a few seconds he remain dazed and confused. He felt dizzy and began to shiver. A few minutes passed and finally he returned to his senses. It was no easy task to stay cool considering the circumstances.

He opened the two smaller chests to reveal jade carvings, royal calligraphy and paintings on scrolls. He saw a shell-shaped white jade cup, and an imperial lion seal which was the emperor's personal mark and sign of authority. More jade artefacts, gold coins, and solid gold figurines. Hilton was alert not to touch any of the valuable items, fearful he might contaminate the contents. He stepped back to view the splendour of all the open chests. He stood motionless, overcome by the moment.

Hilton felt himself floating back in time. To the time of the pirates. He envisioned their battles at sea, cannons blasting, ships on fire, men jumping overboard, and the victors taking spoils back to Cheung Chau. They docked at the small cove below and made the difficult journey up the hillside to the hidden entrance of the treasure cave. They lowered their prized possessions into the basket under the strict supervision of Cheung Po Tsai and only he would know how to access the secret chamber. Piece by piece he would record his inventory and arrange the chests so he could admire the booty he had plundered from merchant ships and those of the Imperial Chinese navy. Hilton could almost see the ghost of Cheung Po Tsai sitting on the middle chest, draped in his pirate flag, fondling the emperor's jewels, applauding and saying, 'Well done, well done . . . you two kids would make great pirates.'

Hilton was brought out of his trance by the loud, echoing sound of clapping hands directly behind him. Had Cheung Po Tsai come back from the dead, seeking revenge or did he just want to protect his treasure? Was Hilton's head to be next on the chopping block? Was Cookie right? Had the ghost of Cheung Po Tsai come back to reclaim his treasure? Hilton trembled, took a deep breath, regained his courage enough to turn and face the unknown.

Chapter 16

THE ENTRANCE TO THE CAVE, Cookie had been AT surprised from behind and had no chance to react or defend herself. Her assailants must have heard her voice echoing inside the cave entrance, leading them right to her. Fatty and Chopstick now had her hands and feet bound with rope, remembering the painful kicks she dealt them at the KCR station. They used the towel Hilton had affixed to the bush, to silence her by tying it around her mouth. Fatty found her cell phone and threw it to the rocks below. Hilton had no idea what was happening above. Cookie had no way to warn him Big Brother had gone down in the basket.

Big Brother moved closer to Hilton, continuing his sarcastic applause.

'Well done my young detective,' praised Big Brother. 'Well done.'

'Where's my sister?' demanded Hilton. 'You better not hurt her, you do and I'll kill you.'

Big Brother motioned to Hilton with his walking stick.

'How very noble,' replied Big Brother. 'No one is going to get hurt unless you get stupid, understand.'

It did not appear to Hilton that this man had a gun or any other weapon. Hilton began to move forward. Big Brother stuck out his walking stick halting Hilton in his tracks.

'I'd stay right there if I were you,' cautioned Big

Brother, 'My friend here is packing ten thousand Volts.'

Big Brother touched the stone surface with his stick and loud crackling sounds were followed by a series of flying sparks. Hilton backed off. Big Brother went over to the ancient chests and peered inside them one by one, while keeping close watch on Hilton.

'Exquisite, simply breathtaking,' remarked big Brother. 'You just happened to be in the right place at the right time. If you had arrived at that shop a few minutes later that spyglass would have been in my possession where it rightfully belongs. I spent eight years tracking down this treasure. I knew the spyglass contained a map that held the key to untold riches.

'I finally tracked it to that shop in Stanley. Then out of nowhere you came along. Who could believe it? A couple of kids end up with my spyglass. You obviously didn't even know what you had. But I have to give you a lot of credit, you figured it out. I am not sure I would have worked it out myself. Maybe it would have taken me another eight years, so for that, I am grateful. But the treasure is mine. Hope you had a good look because you're not likely to see it again.'

Big Brother was looking through the treasure chests while he gloated, keeping Hilton at a safe distance with his electric walking stick. He stopped his inspection and closed the chests.

Big Brother pointed to the smaller chest and motioned for Hilton to grab the leather handle on the side.

'I'll take the other side and we are going to move these chests to the outer entrance,' instructed Big Brother. 'Don't try anything foolish or your sister will suffer. It's a long way down to the bottom of the cave without a rope, keep that in mind.'

Hilton could not take any chances with Cookie's safety. He followed instructions and the two of them eventually got all three treasure chests to the outer chamber and to the edge of the stone platform. Big Brother motioned for Hilton to step back and he complied.

'Oh, by the way, give me your mobile phone,' demanded Big Brother. 'Hurry up I don't have all day.'

Hilton slowly rummaged through his backpack, stalling for time. Locating the phone he passed it over to big Brother who threw it out the doorway. It sailed into the darkness and they heard it smash on the rocky surface far below.

'Fatty, Chopstick, hold the ropes tightly,' yelled Big Brother. 'I am going to load three chests in the basket and I want you two to bring them up when I tell you, got it.'

'Got it, we got it, we're ready,' replied Fatty's voice echoing from above.

Big Brother secured the locks on the chests as best he could and began to push them over the edge and into the basket. One, two, three, they fell against each other, filling the basket to capacity. Fatty and Chopstick could feel the weight increasing. Big Brother finally gave the order.

'Pull, pull hard you two, harder,' shouted Big Brother.

Soon the basket began to slowly rise out of sight. Big Brother looked over at Hilton who stared at him angrily.

'We should keep in touch,' said Big Brother. 'I could use a smart young man like you.'

'Dream on,' replied Hilton sharply. 'Do you really think you can get away with this?'

'Watch me, just watch me,' replied Big Brother.

'My sister better be okay or I'll hunt you down to the ends of the earth, that's a promise,' stated Hilton.

'I give you my word, in fact I'll have her sent down to keep you company,' he replied.

After several minutes the empty basket reappeared at the treasure chamber's entrance.

'Oh, I almost forgot, give me my spyglass,' demanded Big Brother. 'It's mine, not yours.'

Hilton reluctantly removed the spyglass from his waist pack, then hesitated.

'Your sister, remember,' said Big Brother, pointing upwards. Hilton tossed it over gently and Big Brother caught it, looked at it, and put it in his pocket.

Big Brother carefully climbed in the basket. He tugged on the ropes and Hilton watched him slowly ascend. A few minutes later the basket reappeared with Cookie sitting there, tied up and gagged. Hilton pulled the basket towards the entrance and dragged Cookie to the safety of the landing area. He quickly untied her and she jumped to her feet, shaking with anger.

'Let's get those guys, I am going to kill them. They trashed my mobile phone,' she screamed. 'Do you know how much stuff I had programmed in there!'

'Are you okay?' asked Hilton. 'Did they hurt you?'

'No I'm fine, but it was three against one, and from behind, no fair, bunch of gutless scumbags,' she continued.

'Did you see the three wooden chests?' asked Hilton.

'Yeah, I saw those morons dragging them out of the cave entrance,' replied Cookie. 'You found it, the treasure, you found it! I knew it was still on this island, I knew it. In the other cave, remember I told you I saw the ghost of Cheung Po Tsai. I forgot to mention, when he put his sword through the cave wall there was an image of three chests, just like those ones. That's the treasure all right, the real treasure. We have to get it back.'

'First we have to get out of here,' said Hilton.

Hilton tugged at the two ropes attached to the pulley which brought the basket up and down the shaft of the cave. The ropes gave way and the basket went crashing to the bottom of the dark expanse. The ropes had been cut.

Cookie pointed out the other two ropes attached to a second pulley. They were not attached to any basket and may have served some other purpose. There was no way to tell if they were safe and were about three metres away, dangling close the corridor wall on the opposite side of the dark cavern.

Fatty and Chopstick struggled to drag the three chests out of the mouth of the cave and onto the narrow pathway leading down to the cove. The wooden containers were too heavy to carry back towards town and they surely had to stay out of the public eye. Big Brother eyed the coastline below.

'Chopstick, go back to town, get a small boat and come around to that little beach down there,' ordered Big Brother.

'All the way back to town, find a boat, got it, right?'

'Get going dummy, you two are driving me insane,' snapped big Brother.

Chopstick noted the position of the small bay and headed back towards the town centre.

'Should I return the rickshaw?' asked Chopstick.

'Get out of here you fool,' yelled Big Brother.

'They charge by the hour,' added Fatty.

'Idiots, I am surrounded by idiots,' yelled Big Brother.

Back at the beach barbecue, all Hilton's friends had everything prepared. They were just waiting for the guest of honour to show up.

Rico and his friends were passing by, looking very dejected and truly humbled by today's events. Sammie and Echo pointed in their direction and T-Rex and Zack walked over to head them off. Rico was ready to accept his quota of jeers and sarcasm from Hilton's friends. Rico's gang intercepted them. They were ready for action if things got rough.

'Rico, tough luck out there today,' said T-Rex.

'Just wasn't your day man,' added Zack.

'Why don't you guys join us, we have tons of food and lots to drink,' said T-Rex motioning them to follow him.

Rico and his friends were totally taken by surprise at the invitation. Rico thought for a few seconds.

'Sounds like a plan,' replied Rico cautiously. He motioned for his friends to follow.

They all made their way over to the barbecue area and joined the group.

'T-Rex, give Hilton and Cookie a ring,' said Zack. 'We're all starving. It's not like Hilton to be late for a meal.'

T-Rex took out his phone and punched in the numbers. The call went immediately to voicemail. He tried many times with the same result. He checked his watch and tried again. They should have been here by now, he thought. It wasn't like Hilton to be late. After all, this was his victory celebration. T-Rex told Zack that Hilton's phone must be dead, or maybe had no signal. Echo tried to call Cookie, with the same result. Where were those guys? This was not a good sign. Something was definitely wrong.

Chapter 17

HILTON AND COOKIE KNEW their only chance to escape was to get hold of the ropes on the other side of the cavern and see if those dusty cords could support their weight. Then they would have a chance to climb back to the entrance above. Hilton ran back to the treasure chamber and came out with a torch pole. He put out the fire and took the nylon rope from his backpack. At one end he tied the rope, which was about seven metres long. On the other end of the pole, he securely tied his boomerang. Cookie caught on to what Hilton was doing and helped tighten the knots.

Hilton held an end of the rope and tossed the pole across the abyss. The boomerang hit the ropes and Hilton quickly pulled the rope back, hoping to hook one of the vertical lines, sort of like spear fishing. His first attempt failed, not even close, and he knew this was not going to be easy. Hilton tried several more times and was getting frustrated and handed it over to Cookie. Maybe she had a better touch. But she struggled with the awkwardly weighted pole, finding it impossible to balance and control. Hilton came up with a new technique, and Cookie handed him the pole.

The two ropes went right to the bottom of the cave floor. If he could get the boomerang hook around the back of the ropes, let the torch pole fall, then let the weight of the pole hold the ropes in position, then maybe he could draw them back towards him. The first few attempts failed but it appeared he had the right idea. Finally he got the hook around the ropes and the weight of the pole bought the ropes forward. With a gentle touch, Hilton slowly pulled the nylon cord towards himself. He remembered fishing with Grandpa and reeling in his catch. He grabbed the end of the pole and slowly brought them home. Cookie eagerly grabbed the ropes as they arrived. He untied his boomerang from the torch pole and placed it securely in his belt.

'Alright, we did it,' cheered Cookie. 'Way to go Hilton.'

'Now we have to make sure these ropes can hold our weight,' said Hilton as he gave them a stern tug and then a violent jerk.

'Should be okay,' commented Cookie. 'Let's go Tarzan, the monkeys are getting away.'

Chopstick was huffing and puffing, completely out of breath when he arrived at the harbour. He composed himself and started to look for a boat to rent. It was dinner time and he did not have any luck convincing anyone to get ready to go right away. Finally he got smart and offered a small, thin man three times his normal price to make the ten-minute trip. The man's sampan was very small and very old, but it appeared this was the best Chopstick could do under the circumstances. The boatman agreed and they prepared to leave the harbour.

The man started up the motor and it sputtered and spit as they chugged slowly out of the harbour. Chopstick pointed out the direction and they made a hard right turn. About halfway there, Chopstick concluded that the boat was too small for four men and three boxes. He stood up and unceremoniously pushed the boat owner overboard and took control of the slow-moving boat. The boat owner loudly cursed at Chopstick as he paddled to reach the life preserver Chopstick threw over his shoulder as he sailed off.

Inside the cave, Hilton was ready to try his luck. He wrapped the thick rope around his waist and swung out of the entranceway. He sailed through the air using his feet to buffer his contact with the rock wall on the other side of the shaft. He began to pull himself upward at the same time using his feet to walk up the damp, stone surface. The wall was slippery and it was difficult to make progress. Hilton struggled but was not about to give up any time soon. He dug in his heels and used all his strength to pull himself upward. He was on his way.

Fatty and Big Brother had began the delicate task of getting the three heavy chests down the narrow, slippery pathway to the inlet. One wrong move would take them and the treasure down the hillside and on to the jagged rocks lining the shore. They knelt down on each side of a chest to maintain balance. On their knees, they carefully and slowly guided it down to the tiny bay. They worked at a snail's pace but it was effective. One down, two to go. Wiping the sweat from their foreheads, they ascended the hill and started the procedure over again.

'Where is Chopstick?' Big Brother asked angrily, looking at his watch. 'He's been gone for well over an hour.'

Fatty shrugged and looked out to sea, straining and squinting his eyes trying to locate his partner.

'There he is, over there,' shouted Fatty pointing frantically towards a small boat making its way around the headland.

They both stopped for moment to see Chopstick guiding the boat and waving at them in the distance.

'Where did he find that boat, Toys 'R' Us? What an idiot,' complained Big Brother. 'Hurry up, it'll be dark soon and we won't be able to see where we're going.'

Hilton was making steady progress but was tiring after a very strenuous day. Cookie was getting impatient. There was no way to tell just far away the three men had escaped with the treasure. Would they ever be able to catch them? Hilton had almost reached the stone platform at the entrance to the cave. Just a few more steps.

Fatty and Big Brother had guided the third chest down the slippery slope and onto the beach area. Fatty waved to Chopstick as he was now only a few hundred metres away. They were confident of making a clean getaway. They frantically signalled Chopstick to hurry but the small sampan could not move any faster. Big Brother sat on the large chest thoroughly disgusted with Chopstick.

Hilton finally reached the landing area and shouted down to Cookie: 'Tie the rope around your waist, swing to the other side and start walking up the wall like I did. I'll pull you up.'

Cookie tied on the rope securely and swung out into empty space. She scrambled up the cave wall as Hilton pulled the rope as fast as he could. They knew time was running out. The crooks could already be long gone. Cookie reached the stone platform and now they were both safe. She quickly untied herself and they rushed down the narrow passageway into the bright sunlight.

Hilton pointed down towards the small cove far below.

'Cookie, look . . . down there,' exclaimed Hilton. 'There they are, let's go, quick.'

Chopstick guided the sampan as close as possible to the beach and dropped anchor. He jumped out and the three men lifted the first chest on to their shoulders. They waded into the waist-deep water and placed the chest in the boat. They repeated the procedure and soon had all three treasure chests on board. They carefully climbed in, trying to balance the overloaded vessel. The boat wobbled back and forth before becoming steady. Big Brother scowled at Fatty and Chopstick, showing his displeasure with the way they had handled the whole affair.

Cookie and Hilton began creeping down the narrow pathway, trying to stay low and being as quiet as possible. They were now halfway down and could see the three men had already loaded up the boat and were about to leave.

Suddenly a voice came from the top of the hill, a familiar voice. 'There they are, let's go!'

The twins were surprised by the appearance of T-

Rex. And their other friends were right behind him. Hilton frantically signalled to him to be quiet as he saw the small army swarm over the hilltop and start their way down to meet them. Hilton and Cookie were glad to have reinforcements, but now they had lost the element of surprise. No more sneaking. They started running full speed down the hill to the small cove.

The three men heard the voices from above and looked landward. They saw the stream of teenagers pour over the top of the hill and head down the pathway. Then they saw Cookie and Hilton racing down the narrow strip of land towards them.

'How did those brats get out of there?' shouted Big Brother angrily. 'I should have thrown him to the bottom of the cave. What a time to be Mister Nice guy. Let's get out of here. Hurry up!'

Hilton and Cookie had reached the sandy cove and their friends were now about 50 metres behind them, and coming fast. Hilton heard the motor start up and had to act quickly. The heavily-loaded sampan turned away in slow motion. The three men only had room to stand and tried desperately to balance themselves in the choppy waters. Hilton took the boomerang from his belt, took aim and threw it.

Chopstick ducked to avoid being struck. He grabbed onto Fatty and they both went overboard. The boomerang flew over their heads, circled and came back, landing in the shallow water close to Hilton's feet.

'Help, help!' cried Fatty grabbing onto Chopstick. 'I can't swim.'

'You can't swim?' replied Chopstick. 'I can't swim. Help, help!'

The two men thrashed around in the ocean, taking in great mouthfuls of sea water. Panic was setting in but Big Brother was not about to go to his helpless nephews' rescue. They were on their own. He had no time to waste if he was going to make his escape with the treasure. With a lightened load, the boat started to move faster.

Hilton recovered the boomerang, rubbed his lucky shark tooth, took aim and threw it again with all his might. He could see the shock in Big Brother's eyes as it rocketed towards him. Big Brother covered his face, the boomerang swerved and struck the small motor of the sampan with tremendous force. It was a direct hit. The boomerang shattered on impact. The motor stuttered several times then stopped all together. It had given up the ghost. Big Brother fell back onto the chests, recovered his balance and tried to restart the engine. He toyed with the throttle but his efforts were fruitless. The small boat was now rocking back and forth. Hilton and Cookie looked at each other, threw off their backpacks and dove into the water.

A few seconds later their friends made it to the beach, and all the boys jumped into he water, eager to assist Hilton and Cookie.

Big Brother could see the swimmers heading for the boat. He looked around and picked up an oar. He started to paddle with all his might.

Hilton and Cookie were getting closer. Without a motor he could not possibly outrun the two school swim team champions. They were only a metre from the boat when Big Brother drew out his electric walking stick and pointed it in their direction. They stopped dead in the water.

'Don't come any closer or I'll use this,' shouted Big Brother.

'Electricity and water don't mix, you should have learned that in school,' shouted Hilton.

Someone swam up quickly from behind as the twins dove underwater. They disappeared beneath the surface and came up on the other side of the boat. The three teenagers started rocking the boat back and forth. Big Brother lost his battle to keep his balance and went overboard. His walking stick flew from his hand and crackled and sparkled as it hit the water, then sank to the ocean floor.

Hilton and Cookie looked over at the third person who had helped them out. Rico, the last person they expected to see. Hilton gave him an approving slap on the shoulder as they watched the rest of their friends swim towards the three crooks. The swimmers now had the panicking trio surrounded. They grabbed hold of them and kept them afloat.

From over the hilltop, they heard an ear-shattering, stuttering roar.

A police helicopter rose from behind the crest of the hill, circled, and started to descend on the scene. It stayed a safe distance as not to cause waves that might engulf the swimmers. Then came the high-pitched sound of sirens. Two Marine Police launches quickly sped around the end of the island and headed in their direction. Julien Chan stood on the bow of the police boat along with ten other officers. He motioned for the captain to cut the engines and the two boats settled into position. The helicopter hovered overhead and Julien quickly assessed the situation. He realised none of the teenagers were in danger and they had everything under control.

Hilton swam over to where T-Rex had collared the gasping Big Brother.

'I think you have something that belongs to me,' insisted Hilton reaching into Big Brother's sports jacket pocket.

He extracted the spyglass and used it to splash some water into Big Brother's angry face. 'Crime doesn't pay,' offered Hilton. 'See you when you get out of prison in about a hundred years.'

Hilton gave T-Rex a thumbs-up, then swam back to Cookie.

The three culprits were gathered up and taken on board the second cruiser and handcuffed. The small sampan was towed back to Cheung Chau Harbour and returned to the shaken but grateful owner who had been rescued by the Marine Police on their way to the cove. The treasure chests were loaded onto Julien's police boat along with all the teenagers, then headed back to the small cove.

On the boat, Julien wrapped a towel around Cookie and placed his hand on Hilton's shoulder. The twins were out of breath and happy to see everyone was all right.

'You sure you don't want a ride back to the harbour?' asked Julien. 'You must all be exhausted.'

'We have to return our bikes,' replied Hilton.

'Of course,' said Julien proudly.

'Dad, are we glad to see you,' said Cookie.

'She's not kidding. Good timing dad. We were just cleaning up a little ocean pollution, good for the environment you know,' smiled Hilton pointing in the direction of the three men.

'How did you two ever figure out where the treasure was?' asked Julien. 'You two are really remarkable.'

'No problem dad,' replied Cookie. 'I figured everything out and Hilton tried to get us both killed, simple as that.' Cookie smiled and put the towel over her head, hiding from Hilton.

Julien smiled and shook his head in disbelief. He was truly amazed at the day's events.

'When you told me you were going back to the lookout pavilion, and not joining the barbecue, I knew you two had found something,' said Julien.

'Thanks for the note Hilton, that was very smart. Then when T-Rex phoned I knew my suspicions were correct. I knew something was wrong,' continued Julien.

'I recognised Big Brother on the ferry coming over here. His real name is Wu Feng-feng, calls himself Dr. Wu. We have been trying to build a case against him for a long time. He has been selling ancient Chinese artefacts on the black market. He also acquires these relics, has them duplicated, and sells the fakes to unknowing collectors. You two helped bring his little empire to a grinding halt and it looks like you have a boatload of real pirate treasure as well. Quite a day's work.'

'Thanks you guys,' said Hilton turning to his friends. 'Great to see you all, sorry we were late for

154

the barbecue.'

'All for one and one for all, brother,' shouted Zack and T-Rex.

'I'm hungry, it must be barbecue time,' said Cookie cheerfully.

The boat slowed near the small cove and the group of tired teenagers got off. Hilton and Cookie stopped and took a long look around. They were never going to forget this adventure. The group started back up the hillside path.

'Your mother and I will see you later,' said Julien waving from the deck of the boat.

The large engines of the police cruisers started up, roaring like hungry lions. The watercraft turned gracefully, heading back to their base in Cheung Chau Harbour. Hilton and Cookie ran to join their friends.

Several weeks later, at an official presentation the whole adventure seemed very surreal, like a dream. It was still difficult to believe, this fairy-tale ending was real.

At the ceremony, the Hong Kong and Beijing government officials agreed that part of the emperor's treasure would remain on display at he Palace Museum in Beijing. The other part would be on display at the Museum of History in Hong Kong. Every six months they would alternate the historic items so all could witness the entire collection.

For their initiative and bravery, Hilton and Cookie each received a full scholarships to the University of Hong Kong upon graduation from secondary school along with individual trust funds of an undisclosed amount. The Chief Executive presented Hilton and Cookie each with a Silver Medal for Bravery. They were extremely honoured but it was hard to believe they were really modern-day treasure hunters and crime solvers.

T-Rex, Zack, Sammie, and Echo were invited to join the family for a celebration dinner and after enduring the photographers' frenzy they made a unified exit.

As they walked out of Government House, Cookie spoke up about something she'd been thinking about for a while. 'I know you don't really believe I saw a ghost, Hilton. But it is true, and you know, we never would have found the treasure without his help.'

'But if it was Cheung Po Tsai's ghost, why would he want us to find his treasure?' asked Hilton, humouring her.

'He knew Big Brother was getting close. If he'd found it, the treasure would be broken up and sold. Nothing would be left to remind anyone of who Cheung Po Tsai was and what he did. For a ghost, that's worse than death. Now there will be hundreds of visitors every day to look at the "Treasure of Cheung Po Tsai" exhibits. His place in history is secure.'

Hilton was still sceptical. 'It was pure luck. If I hadn't gone to the junk shop in Stanley that day. . . .' 'And why did you go? The shark. The *Ghost Shark*. . . .'

'So, what's next for Hong Kong's newest superheroes?' joked T-Rex, putting his arms around Hilton and Cookie.

'Yeah, maybe you two should start your own hip-hop group or something,' laughed Zack.

Hilton and Cookie immediately looked at each other with raised eyebrows. They smiled and nodded. 'Now there's an idea.'

'The Hip-hop Twins are alive and well,' exclaimed Cookie.

Hilton dug out his MP3 player from his inner sport jacket pocket and turned it up full blast so everyone could hear it from the overloaded ear phones. The friends began showing off dance moves as they made their way to the waiting vehicles.

'Yeahhhhhhhh, that's right,' the group shouted together raising their hands in the air moving joyously to the faint sounds of Hilton's MP3 player. 'Let's get this party started . . . get started . . . get started . . . let's party . . . let's get it started . . . it's party time . . . no time to rest . . . it's party time . . . cause we're the best . . . let's bounce y'all . . . let's bounce.'

Historical note

THE SPANISH MAIN, the Barbary Coast, and the intoxicating Caribbean were not the only locations plagued by pirates centuries ago.

The South China Sea, and in particular the outlying islands that make up what is now the territory of Hong Kong, played host to possibly the largest contingent of pirates ever to sail the high seas. Some 40,000 pirates and an imposing armada of over 600 ships patrolled passages along the trade routes to China. The pirates regularly raided the merchant ships of Britain and Portugal, as well as vessels from the Chinese Imperial fleet.

Cheung Po Tsai was the fearless leader of these cutthroats. A mere teenager when forced to join the pirate brigade, his Red Flag band controlled the pirate hordes. His reputation became legendary as he and his buccaneers instilled fear amongst the local villagers, and demanded respect and payment from all who dare sail into their waters.

Along with his wife, the Dragon Lady, he commanded possibly one of the largest, and maybe the most competent collection of seafaring scoundrels ever assembled. These pirates were intelligent, ruthless, and feared nothing except the wrath of Cheung Po Tsai.

The pirates extorted gold and supplies from the merchant ships in return for safe passage. The pirate fleet eventually did battle with the combined naval heavyweights of Britain, Portugal, and China as these nations grew increasing angry at the pirates' aggression and relentless greed. The seas ran red with blood and the hungry sharks feasted on many a hapless sailor. Nine days later the pirates proclaimed victory.

Great fortunes were acquired by the pirate bands and much of the treasure is still unaccounted for. The territory's 240-plus islands provided a myriad of hiding places and legend has it that untold wealth is out there waiting to be discovered.

The Mystery of Hong Kong's Pirate Island
"X" Marks the Spot Prizes

First:	$ 300 USD	or	£200 Sterling
Second:	$ 150 USD	or	£100 Sterling
Third:	$ 50 USD	or	£30 Sterling

"X" Marks the Spot Treasure Hunt

Decipher the Clues provided and tell us where you think the treasure is buried…savvy!

CLUES

After his execution, his body was left to hang in a cage over the Thames River in 1701.

Notorious captain, whose legend was rekindled in the novel "Treasure Island", by Robert Louis Stevenson.

May have buried treasure on an island or two along the eastern seaboard of North America.

Rumoured to have been the pirate responsible for constructing an intricate money pit, and hiding a vast treasure here…"X"…where is it?

Each entry must be forwarded with the proof of purchase. One entry per each proof of purchase.

Name – Age – Home City – E-mail – must be included on the front of your submission. Forward via e-mail as MS Word or Rich Text Format attachment to contact@gstuartnakay.com

All entrants will be automatically enrolled as a member in: "Evolution X", a club where imagination has no limitations.

Correct entries will go into a "Lucky Draw", and the winners will be posted online at www.gstuartnakay.com Lucky Draw will be in reverse order with 3rd prize being drawn first.